ELECTRIC LITERATURE

COVER

Within a Given Day
IN: 52 X 42 mixed media on stretched canvas

Clayton Brothers
Rob Clayton & Christian Clayton

Clayton Brothers Studio
2942 Honolulu avenue
La Crescenta, CA. 91214

PHONE : 818.541.0750
WEB SITE : www.claytonbrothers.com
EMAIL : requestinfo@claytonbrothers.com

ELECTRIC LITERATURE NO.2

Andy Hunter
Co-publisher, Editor-in-Chief

Scott Lindenbaum
Co-publisher, Editor

Jeff Price
Associate Editor

Molly Auerbach & Anna Prushinskaya
Editorial Assistants

Bill Smith | designsimple.com
Designer

Katie Byrum
Copy Editor

Stephen Aubrey, Stephen Douglas, Anna DeForest, Noia Efrat, Nora Fussner,
Erin Harte, Jennifer Kikoler, Cristina Moracho, Felise Nguyen, Chloe Plaunt,
Christine Rath Selhi, Helen Rubinstein, Richard Santos, Evelyn Spence,
Elizabeth Stevens, Raina Washington, Anna Wiener, Pia Wilson
Readers

Special Thanks
Jonathan Ashley, Nick Dewitt, Martha Colburn, Jo Dery, Jim Shepard,
Luca Dipierro, Anna Cory-Watson, Ron Charles, Robert Cohen,
Peggy and Richard Price, MFD, Alison Elizabeth Taylor, Brian Lindenbaum,
Bruce Lindenbaum, Barry Roseman, Alan Roseman, Jordan Holberg,
Larry Benowich, Rick Moody, Josh Henkin, Elliot Holt, Ben George,
Daniel Grandbois, Catherine Bohne, Helen Phillips, Kyle Semmel,
Shya Scanlon, Matthew Korahais, Fiona Maazel

Electric Literature is published bimonthly by Electric Literature, LLC.
325 Gold St. Suite 303, Brooklyn, NY 11201.
Email: editors@electricliterature.com. Copyright 2009 by Electric Literature.
Authors hold the rights to their individual works. All rights reserved.

ISBN 0982498012

For subscriptions, submission information, or to advertise,
visit our website at **electricliterature.com**

CONTENTS

THE COMEDIAN

Colson Whitehead

One

time on a talk show, before he made the change in his comedy, the comedian was asked why he started telling jokes. He took a sip from his mug and responded that he just wanted some attention. As a child he'd felt unseen. He was a handsome baby (photographs confirm) but his impression was that no one cooed at him or went cross-eyed to make him smile. Common expressions of affection, such as loving glances, approving grins, and hearty *that-a-boy*s, eluded him. His mother told him, Hush, now, when he came to her with his needs or questions and he frowned and padded off quietly. He received a measly portion of affirmation from grandparents, elderly neighbors, and wizened aunts who never married, folks who were practically in the affirmation-of-children business. In kindergarten, he was downright appalled to find the bullies stingy with noogies and degrading nicknames. The comedian believed that he was unseen, overlooked, and not-perceived to a greater extent than other people were unseen, overlooked, and not-perceived, when in actuality he was overlooked as much as everyone else, he just felt it more keenly. The talk show host asked him what his first joke was. He said he didn't remember, but he must have liked what happened because he did it again.

The boy practiced and practiced. In the bathroom down the hall, he made funny faces before the white hexagonal tile; he devised oddball catch-phrases and made unlikely connections between seemingly dissimilar objects and phenomena. When he later shoe-horned these observations into conversation, people laughed. He experimented with metaphor and figurative language. Like, when a mouse died in the walls and no one could get to it, he said, That smells like a hundred Roger farts. They were having holiday dinner, the far-flung generations, and the vulgarity cracked everyone up. He broke it down later, staring at the ceiling of his room while the grownups whooped it up in the living room. A familiar situation disrupted by an unexpected and forbidden element produced laughter. The smell of the decomposing mouse was not one Roger fart, but a hundred. Exaggeration was key. Exaggeration was a kind of truth-telling, and it made people laugh. If he made someone chuckle or snicker, he took notes and tried to recreate the circumstances later. Cousin Roger never forgave the comedian this humiliation, his later enthusiasm for his relative's success in his annual Xmas letter notwithstanding.

The comedian expanded his act. One day he decided he needed weapons. Other people were an army straying into his territories and this sent him fashioning defenses before the bathroom mirror. He gathered specific putdowns for use against his friends and family in case they suddenly turned on him, which happened from time to time. He stole jokes from comics he saw on television and didn't give credit. Years later he'd make ridiculous apologies to these men, who were flattered to be remembered and boasted of their influence on him to their grandchildren on their infrequent visits. When his fifth grade teacher named him Class Clown, he knew it wasn't a foolhardy plan after all, this strategy of getting seen. Look at me, look at me.

The comedian learned how to get girls by making them laugh and blush. You'd see him whisper in a girl's ear and she'd giggle and shake her head in sweet outrage. Guys who really wanted to beat him up were disarmed by some weird baboon face of his and forgot all about it. He got into the local college and joined an improvisational comedy troupe his first semester. The group's fliers were everywhere, stapled to utility poles and taped to the doors of lecture halls, and were much better designed than those of other campus societies, like the ones from the a cappella groups. How strange it was, he thought, to be in an a cappella group, and advertise it.

Improv was not his forte. Group interaction in general, frankly. The audience yelled out words—Cantaloupe! Rooster! Watchfob!—and it was their job to construct a jokey situation incorporating them. They kidnapped these mundane things from the familiar and smuggled them to the realm of the absurd. Success was measured by the distance between the original context and the new, alien context of the sketch. The comedian, however, did not believe that things had to travel very far to be funny or sad. You could look at pretty much anything and say, How laughable, or, What a pity. The rest of the troupe liked his sensibility, the wit he'd exhibited during tryouts, but were perplexed by his behavior. They'd set him up perfectly and he'd just stand there playing pocket pool. They parted ways after Halloween weekend.

He went solo. He practiced, and his bits eventually became routines. At open mikes he did impressions of a previous generation's celebrities. They

The Comedian

were really impressions of other people's impressions, stuff he got from television. Whenever he needed to stretch out a set and riff for a few minutes, he could rely on the voices of these dead inside him. The comedian developed a character named Danny the Dentist, who liked to interrogate his patients about weighty matters while their mouths were stuffed with metal and latex. As Danny parsed their grunts—"I totally agree, never let an encyclopedia salesman use your commode on a weekend"—the humor derived from the contrast between the patients' nonsense syllables and his extravagant interpretations. Danny the Dentist spoke a language beyond the audience's understanding. Looking at it one way, it was a kind of commentary on the comedian's lot—to translate between the world as it is and the world as people perceive it. The character caught on, and in a few years he'd do Danny on variety shows and cable programs. When they bring out the old footage for the occasional documentary on the history of comedy, or a ranking of the top twenty-five stand-ups according to a poll, it's always a shock to see Danny. It's like hearing about some backward medieval practice. You can't believe people used to live like that.

He got his diploma because he didn't want to let anyone down and because a graduation ceremony was an opportunity to get attention from those he needed attention from. He wasn't disappointed, with regards to their attendance. His family showed up and they all went out to lunch. They asked, What are you going to do now?

He kept hitting the clubs and expanding his routine. He cut jokes. Why did he ever think that corny bit was funny? This is my new style, he told himself, and six months later the new style was out the window and a newer strain dominated his set list. The old jokes testified to how stupid he'd been. But if people laughed, what did that say about people? Local comedy clubs gave him some slots and he started hanging out with his peers. The other comics weren't threatened. He wasn't exactly pushing the boundaries. Like, in one of his bits, three representatives of different religious faiths were trapped in an isolated place where their differences were struck into sharp relief. Or, he closed his act with the observation that one group of people tended to do things differently than another group of people, and he listed a few examples. Plodder, the other comics said. Word came down that a scout from the big late-night talk show was going to check out "the scene" and everybody worried and fussed. The scout frowned throughout the comedian's set. A month later, when they went out for drinks after his appearance on the talk show, the scout told him, I try to laugh on the inside.

This was the start of his celebrity. They flew him around the country. He got a manager and learned how to pack efficiently. He didn't have what you called a distinctive style, but he ran the bases and that was enough, even if they had a hard time remembering his name afterward. He played bigger and bigger rooms. A screenwriter got in touch about writing a spec script based on one of the comedian's characters, the Limo Driver. The Limo Driver was always sticking his nose into his passengers' affairs, hilariously clueless about his lack of boundaries. The comedian met the screenwriter in a coffee shop and they brainstormed. He was surprised that there were professions more desperate and sad than his own. He told the screenwriter that it was probably a bad idea. When offered cameo gigs on sitcoms and small independent features, he passed. He didn't like make-believe. Even when the Limo Driver exaggerated some human weakness, he didn't think he was stretching the truth.

He enjoyed the money and the flattery that was thousands of people listening to his every word. His girlfriend moved into his condo, and this was a period he always looked back fondly upon, even though it didn't work out in the end for a lot of reasons, not the least of which was all the travel. He was never around. Every new city and gig was a chance to get it right finally, and nothing could compete with that.

When he thought back on the day he changed his comedy, he never came up with an explanation. He'd been on a good run, and it was just another gig. He was in an American city of a certain size, the kind where if you were a B-list comedian there was really only one venue for you to perform in, and he was performing on its stage. He was halfway through his act, up there doing Danny. Danny the Dentist was elbow deep in the mouth of a German tourist who'd been in a wiener schnitzel accident (the bit had a rather long and baroque setup). As the comedian said the words he'd said a hundred times before, he heard a high-pitched whistling in his ears. No one else seemed to notice it, and he thought for a minute that it was another one of his mysterious physical or mental symptoms, but quickly understood that it was more than that. He stopped speaking (his mouth had continued the routine, such was his professionalism) and looked into the audience. They were a hive of faces before him, still and attentive, arranged like hexagonal tile in a bathroom. The comedian said

The Comedian

the words that popped into his head: "If I had known what little came from talking to other people, I never would have learned how to speak." The microphone dispatched these words into the sound system and into the void of the auditorium. And then they laughed. They laughed for a nice comfortable while. The comedian resumed his act (poor Danny, poor German tourist), but he knew something had changed.

The next night, and the night after that, a thousand miles away, he shared another one of his confidences with the audience, and they ate it up. He shared more and more confidences with the people who came to see him and after two weeks they had become his whole act, the confidences crowding out Danny the Dentist, the Limo Driver, the Stuttering Hooker, stepping on their lines and hogging the spotlight until they stopped showing up. Out of habit he persisted with the tools of the trade—the crooked eyebrows, head wagging, and shrugs—not trusting people to understand his new message. But they did understand. One by one the gestures fell away, he left them behind in city after city until his act was unadorned by the traditional flourishes of comedy, the nudges and cues the jester uses to urge the audience to laughter. They were no longer necessary.

He couldn't walk down the street anymore. The first concert film broke a lot of records and he sold a ton of CDs—although not as many as you'd think. He made his millions performing live, recordings failing to capture the essence of his new routine. As with a lot of non-traditional humor, *you had to be there*, but the recordings were still popular among those who'd seen him in person and, late at night, needed to relive his confidences. Even when robbed of indefinable energies, the sound of his voice helped bring them back. When other comics tried to rip off his style, they discovered that the comedian was impossible to copy. Something was lost. It was in him.

His new shtick fell into two subject areas:

Everything Is Terrible

People Are Disappointing

To his notion of the Terrible, there were a variety of responses. Some were relieved. If everything is terrible, then the only thing distinguishing one idea, object, or course of action from another is its degree of terribleness. This, one might say, is obviously much more terrible than that, and once you made the calculation, you were good to go. It saved a lot of time. Others were grateful. Let's stop pretending, the comedian said.

Isn't it all so tedious and wearying, pretending that the world is other than that which it is, namely, terrible? We walk around, jibber at each other, share our dreams in order to change the subject, but we all know what's going on, we know what we're avoiding with all this food, fucking, weekend getaways, and *try some of this, you'll like it*. Now there was this man before them just saying it: Things are terrible. They've been terrible for a long time. In fact, they've always been terrible, and the more people there are in the world, implementing their awful imaginations, the more rapidly things get more terrible.

For some of the folks leaning forward in the rows out there, he was the perfect older brother or sister or parent they'd always been waiting for, the one who set them straight, told them how to do it, reserving all the mistakes for themselves, sparing us.

People Are Disappointing needs no elaboration.

Observational humor was a sturdy genre. "*Did you ever notice* this minor, everyday aspect of modern life that I will now blow up to absurd proportion?" "*Why is it that* this familiar situation, when I describe it in a certain way, is the apotheosis of life's tribulations?" But the comedian's new brand required no rhetorical shenanigans. His observations did not need to be massaged. They required only to be shared. For so many years the comedian had believed that what he called the "lack of attention" had been part of a sadness particular to himself, when in fact it was universal. Everyone hid it. No one spoke of it. Until now.

He was the only guy I know, recalled one of his contemporaries, who didn't have any hecklers.

The comedian adjusted to his new fame the best he could. Many performers describe a rush or exhilaration following a show, an ecstatic quickening of the body's processes. Not the comedian. Before he changed his comedy, sure, he was pumped that people had listened to him and seen him, thus proving that he did, in fact, exist. But after his new routines he experienced none of that. He walked off stage but could not help feeling that he was still on stage, with a glass of water and a wooden stool and nothing else. Surrounded by darkness. He got used to it. Members of the service industry, such as waiters and dry cleaners, marveled at how polite the comedian was, what a generous tipper. You're a different person on stage, they said, and he thought, No. After a lifetime of the reverse, that's the real me up there and the rest of the time I'm performing. Here, he captured a feeling common to many artists in other disciplines, although he was loathe to call himself an artist. He thought he was simply telling the truth, and that's not art, is it?

The years passed. He had a good run, but eventually the novelty of his confidences wore off. That's the way it goes. He still sold out the house, but the lovely enthusiasm of that early wave was long gone. One day he called it quits. He didn't announce it or take out a page in the trades or anything. He did the rest of the gigs he'd agreed to do and that was that. He'd said all he had to say. He wasn't hurting for money and for a time he traveled to the places he'd always wanted to go to (He never found an audience overseas until after his death, when he was "discovered" by a noted French critic.). The comedian finally saw the world. It was more or less as he expected, not disappointing in any novel way.

His new life was quiet and he liked it. When he forced himself to admit it, he felt better about things, having got it all off his chest. There had never been anything setting him apart from other people. The audiences proved it. They had been made of the same stuff all along. He chose an unlikely spot to retire, a small town up the coast where he eventually shacked up with a woman who had her own business selling shawls and quilts to summer people. They got along okay. He'd played in the town once, long before, when he was just starting out. It seemed like the whole town showed up that night, filling the old theater and chuckling and applauding. It was the kind of place where people know that life is hard and sometimes what we need at the end of a long day, most of all, is a good laugh. ▣

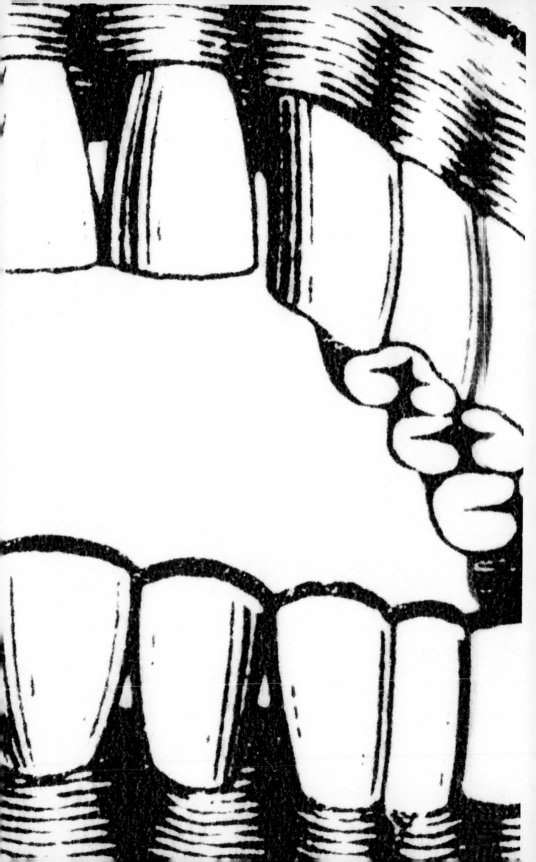

LOVE

Stephen O'Connor

Three

days before Christmas, Alice's college housemate fell over dead of a cerebral hemorrhage while cross-country skiing. At the memorial service, on a frigid Saturday in early January, ten people, Alice among them, crowded the dais of a Unitarian church near Boston to speak to a gathering that the tall-windowed, fog-gray room made seem pathetically small. Alice told the story of an afternoon during college, when she and the housemate—Katinka—had polished off a thermos of margaritas in a sunny field, then lay on their backs, talking and looking up at the sky—only half-noticing as a cow moseyed over to them, followed by another and, somewhat later, by a third. It wasn't until the sky began to darken, and they had gotten unsteadily to their feet, that they discovered themselves surrounded by some score of cows, who were standing shoulder-to-shoulder, emitting bovine grunts, and watching them with enormous eyes. "Katinka just walked right up to one of those cows," Alice explained, "and rapped it twice with her knuckle in the middle of its forehead. 'Excuse me, madam,' she said, and the cow promptly backed away so that we might walk past. She was fearless, dear Katinka, which is one of the reasons it is so hard to believe she is not with us now."

Next to speak was a lean, broad-shouldered young man with Slavic cheekbones and wiry black hair that curled crookedly off the top of his head like smoke from a smoldering fire. Alice had not lived in the same city as her old friend for several years, and so did not immediately recognize this young man as Ian, the longest-lasting of Katinka's numerous boyfriends—her "great love," many people said, although she had never been terribly faithful to him and had finally left him for her married thesis advisor. Ian spoke with wit, tenderness, and eloquence, building toward an evocation of a single instant one blustery evening in Providence, when, without knowing it, he was looking into Katinka's eyes for the last time. "For that infinitesimally small particle of duration," he concluded, "there was no such thing as death, only the two of us on a street corner, shivering, smiling, saying goodbye."

As Ian returned to his seat beside Alice, she knew that, should she even glance in his direction, she would start to cry. Nevertheless, throughout the rest of the ceremony, she remained alert to every shifting of his hands and legs, and to his every caught breath and sigh.

«» «» «»

At the reception, glass of wine in hand, Alice went over to Ian. "Oh!" he exclaimed, on hearing her name. "I've always wanted to meet you!"

"Me too," said Alice. She blushed and corrected herself: "I mean, meet you"—although, in fact, Katinka had almost never spoken to her about him.

Alice told Ian that his speech was the only one that had made her cry. Then she asked, "Are you a poet?"

"God no!" He laughed. "I'm a total sell-out!" He wrote copy for an advertising company, he explained, but he loved Czeslaw Milosz, and his speech had been partially cribbed from of one of Milosz's poems.

When Ian asked what Alice did, she said she was a waitress, then added that she had been working on her PhD thesis for six years.

"What's it about?" he asked.

She touched her lips with her fingertips, as if at a terrifying thought. "Oh please! I don't even want to talk about it!"

Ian went to the bar and came back with two refilled glasses. A little later, he and Alice were sitting side-by-side on folding chairs, eating bruschetta and stuffed tomatoes from paper plates balanced on their knees.

Alice was small, thin-wristed, and nearly hipless. She cut her wavy brown hair herself, and it always looked a tangle, even when, as now, she had swept it up in the back, Victorian-style. Her lips were full and so deeply red she never needed lipstick. Her eyes were huge and heron blue. They flitted delightedly over Ian's lean cheeks, aquiline nose, and muscular, expressive mouth, but always fell to her plate when he looked in her direction.

Neither she nor Ian spoke to anyone else the whole evening. When it turned out that they both lived in Brooklyn, he asked, "Do you want a ride? I've got a car."

"That would be lovely," Alice said.

They arrived at her apartment in Greenpoint shortly after one in the morning. She invited him up for coffee and, except for a mid-afternoon brunch, he didn't leave her apartment for thirty-one hours—which is to say, until 7:30 Monday morning, when he had to go to work.

In the weeks that followed, Alice told her friends, "This is it! Ian's the one!" He seemed to feel the same way about her, and she moved permanently into his apartment in Williamsburg four months later.

Her first night in the apartment they got into a fight about who should have the top drawer of the dresser, but after that they settled so smoothly into a domestic routine that Alice sometimes found it hard to believe that this new life of hers was real, that she and Ian weren't just kids pretending to be grown-ups.

With his trim suits, Italian shoes, and six-figure salary, Ian did, in fact, manage a credible impersonation of an adult, whereas Alice, with her thrift shop wardrobe and perpetually depleted bank account, felt stuck in grad student mode. She was particularly humiliated that she couldn't even come close to paying her half of Ian's rent. He would happily have paid the whole rent on his own—which, after all, was what he had been doing before she moved in—but Alice insisted on contributing the same amount that she had paid in Greenpoint, where rents were lower and she'd had two roommates.

"That sounds reasonable," Ian said, the night they reached this agreement. They were at the dinner table, meal over; Alice had cooked. Ian smiled and kissed the top of her head.

For reasons that she didn't fully understand, she wanted to push his face away as he did this. Instead she stood up and carried her plate toward the kitchen. "Help me with the dishes," she said.

It's my damn dissertation! Alice would tell herself during many a grim four AM. It's killing me! Several times over the course of her first two months living with Ian, she dragged her dissertation drafts and notes into her computer's tiny wastebasket, and let her mouse hover over the command "empty trash"—but never went any further. The woman who had struggled so many years with that dissertation was so much more knowledgeable, compassionate, and wise than the waifish waitress in her black miniskirt, or the compulsive smiler who hardly breathed a word at dinner parties she was taken to by her brilliant boyfriend. That woman, Alice believed, was her real, true self—or, at least, the self she would become if only she could finish the dissertation.

One night she went into the living room where Ian was checking his e-mail, sat down beside him on the couch and announced, "I've got something to say." She had been rehearsing this speech for days, and leapt straight into it before she lost her nerve. "I'm quitting my job and I'm going to move up to my father's cabin in the mountains for the summer."

Ian's handsome face alternated between bafflement and hurt.

"I just have to finish my dissertation," she continued. "It's driving me crazy. It's quiet up there. There are no interruptions. I'll be able to concentrate."

"But what about Cape May?" Ian asked, referring to his father and stepmother's offer of their beach house for his two-week vacation.

"I know," Alice said, as if forgoing the Jersey shore caused her real pain (which, in fact, it did, she assured herself). "It's just that I'm turning thirty in September, and I've got to get this dissertation done so that I can start leading my real life."

The pinch of tension between Ian's expressive eyebrows eased somewhat at the words "real life"—a term which, Alice suspected, he understood as being less about her getting an academic, or at least career-like job, than about their having children.

Alice and Ian had not specifically talked about having children together; their relationship was far too new for that. But one of the things that had set them smiling so happily into their mimosas that first brunch after Katinka's memorial service was the discovery that they both loved kids. Ever since, they had been in the habit of voicing a soppy "Aw!" and grinning at each other with one raised eyebrow every time they saw anyone under two-and-a-half feet tall.

"Well, you know," Ian said, twitching his hands helplessly in his lap and attempting a smile. "If you feel you have to do that, then that's what you have to do."

«» «» «»

The cabin was a ten-minute hike off an old logging road, halfway up a mountain. It had two rooms, electricity, running water (but only cold), and an outhouse. Up until his heart attack a year and a half earlier, Alice's father had used the cabin primarily as an escape from married life. For a couple of weeks every summer and most weekends during the fall, he and two or three friends would load up their cars with beer and spend their days stalking the woods around the cabin in camouflage overalls, or fishing off an aluminum skiff on the small lake just downhill.

Alice had only been to the cabin a few times as a little girl, but on each occasion she had felt she was living in a child's paradise. She and her two younger sisters would spend whole days building teepees in the woods out of sticks and bedsheets or playing mermaids down by the lake. Their parents gave them half-hearted warnings, but never actually supervised their play, and hardly seemed to remember they existed, at least as long as they were home for dinner.

What Alice most loved was to explore the woods entirely on her own, sometimes for hours at a time. Never once on any of her expeditions did she encounter another person—neither child nor adult—and so it had been natural for her to feel that every tree, rock, or stream she passed, every vista she looked out over not only existed—in some secret but essential way—for her enjoyment, but, actually, shared in her enjoyment. When she was happy, how could the trees and lake not also be happy? And how was it possible that the mountains did not exult in their own magnificence?

Unfortunately, Alice's mother enjoyed nothing about the cabin, except, perhaps, its extravagant view of the forested slopes and granite peak of Mount Quiddagunk, but that only when her appreciation had been enhanced by sips from the vodka and orange juice she would prepare herself every morning, or from the martinis that her husband would mix for her every evening. She never went for hikes, never fished, or swam. All she ever did in the afternoon was nap, mouth open, snoring. "This place gives me the willies," she used to say—and absolutely refused to take family vacations at the cabin after Alice turned ten.

«» «» «»

Ian was supposed to come up to the cabin every weekend, but cancelled his first visit at the last minute because an important client from Korea was making an unexpected trip to New York and the whole firm had to work late into the night Saturday and Sunday to get a presentation ready.

Alice was disappointed, but not crushed. She had been missing Ian, especially at night, but at the same time her dissertation had been coming along far better than she had ever dared to imagine, and she had worried about how Ian's visit might affect her momentum and confidence. In the end, she hardly gave a thought to his absence, and her work continued to go well, if somewhat more slowly, over the weekend and throughout the ensuing week.

When Ian finally did arrive, just before sunset the following Friday, Alice had a bottle of wine and two glasses waiting on the round picnic table on the deck. She and Ian shared the bottle, watching Quiddagunk go orange and rose, then devoted the whole rest of the night to sex—not eating until two in the morning, when they snacked in bed on apples and peanut butter.

The following afternoon they dragged Alice's father's fishing skiff out from under the deck and carried it down the steep wooded path to the lake. The skiff had benches at either end and a large space between for fishing tackle and coolers of beer. It also had two sets of oars and oarlocks bow and stern, but Alice and Ian decided to share one set and sat side by side on the rear bench. Somewhere near the middle of the lake, an affectionate kiss led to other more serious kisses, then some intra-swimsuit groping, which ended with Alice lying flat on her back in the skiff's puddly middle, her bikini bottom off in some corner. But when Ian hoisted himself up onto his left elbow so that he might wriggle out of his own swimsuit, the shifting of his weight caused the skiff to lurch up on its right side, which, in turn, caused him to topple against the left gunwale and Alice to roll on top of him. After a brief interval of thumps, shouts, and metallic clamor, Alice and Ian found themselves surrounded by murky green and strings of silvery bubbles. Rising to the surface at the same instant, they spotted the skiff floating crookedly, upside down, and both started to laugh.

"Way to go, Romeo!" said Alice, aiming a splash at Ian's head.

"Hey!" protested Ian. "You never told me the boat had an ejection seat!"

They circled each other, splashing and laughing, and every now and then came together for a kiss. Alice still wore her bikini top and tee shirt, but had nothing on below, a state of affairs that had decided advantages for each of them—although Alice did hope her bikini bottom hadn't been lost forever; she'd only brought one swimsuit to the cabin.

«» «» «»

Ian was telling a story about getting bumped overboard while white-water rafting, when Alice noticed that the gunwale on the more uptilted side of the skiff was less than an inch underwater. The slightest of waves—it seemed to her—could lift the gunwale high enough above the surface that the air pocket beneath would gasp free, and the whole boat would roll over and descend to the bottom of the lake.

"Oh my God!" she called out. "The skiff's about to sink!"

Ian looked at the boat, then back at her, his lips and brow screwed up in mock incredulity. "No it's not!"

"It might," she said. "What if the air pocket escapes?"

"That wouldn't make any difference."

"Why not?"

"It just wouldn't."

"How do you know?"

"Because that's the way these things are built. They're unsinkable. They've got these blocks of Styrofoam at either end."

Love

It was true that there was a sealed triangular space at the bow that might have contained a block of Styrofoam, but the stern was entirely open. At best there may have been some Styrofoam under the rear seat, but not nearly enough to keep the skiff afloat.

As Alice mentally debated whether to voice her doubts, Ian said, "Let's flip it over."

"The boat?"

"Yeah. Flip it over. Like a canoe. Back when I was in Boy Scouts, we went on this camping trip and they taught us how to flip an overturned canoe. You have to stretch across the bottom and grab the far side. Something like that."

None of this made sense to Alice. Even if Ian could somehow perform the gravity-defying feat of yanking the far side of the skiff into the air, the near side would only scoop up water as it rolled around underneath—which, at the very least, would swamp the boat.

"I don't know," she said unhappily.

"We can do it!" Ian pulled himself over to the cockeyed craft in two strong strokes. "Come on! It'll work if we both do it."

"I don't know," Alice repeated. "Maybe we should just swim it to shore."

Ian wasn't listening. With a swoop of his arms and a powerful dolphin kick, he flung himself across the upturned bottom of the boat and managed to grab the far side, but only with one hand. "Help me!" he shouted. "You do it too!"

Alice watched in alarm as the near side of the skiff was forced deep below the surface by Ian's weight. In the next instant, he shouted "Shit!" and flopped backwards. She ducked underwater to escape being hit by him, and, when she rose to the surface, saw the skiff floating exactly as crookedly as before and not an inch deeper.

"We have to do this together!" Ian said. He flung himself once again across the bottom of the boat, the muscles on his back and ribs rippling through his sopping tee shirt. Unable to grasp the far gunwale this time, he slipped right back into the water, and, yet again, the skiff bobbed into its cockeyed float.

Alice joined in Ian's next several attempts. She was an excellent swimmer, but far smaller than he and not remotely as strong. The best she could manage was to get her chest onto the near half of the skiff's bottom and to claw at the far half with her fingertips. One time Ian grabbed her by her armpit and thigh and shoved her up onto the overturned boat, but the entire purpose of that exercise seemed to have been to expose her bare butt so that he could give her a not entirely pain-free spanking.

She slipped back into the water and pinched his cheek. "We're not getting anywhere."

"You're right," he said.

In the end they had to do what Alice had suggested at the start: swim the skiff the hundred or so yards back to the shore. At first Ian swam ahead, pulling the boat's dock line, while Alice put her hands against the stern and kicked. But soon they discovered that even a little forward motion caused the skiff's down-sloping bow to cut deep beneath the surface, so they turned the boat around and swam it stern-first—which was only marginally easier.

The second Alice was able to put her feet down on the mucky bottom, she leaned her temple against the skiff's dented hull and panted in sobs, worried that she might have seriously strained her heart. Ian was also panting, but only as if he had climbed a flight of stairs. He waited patiently while Alice regained her breath.

They walked the overturned boat toward the dock until the water was shin-deep. Then, each taking an end, they grunted, lifted the boat into the air, and heaved it over. It flopped onto its belly with a reverberant bang, then skidded sideways like ice in a frying pan, a scrim of peat-peppered water sloshing back and forth under the seats.

No bikini bottom.

"Shit," muttered Alice. And, just at that instant, Ian cried, "Fuck!"

"What's the matter?" she asked.

"The oars!"

Alice looked into the skiff. Both sets were gone, even the pair they had never bothered to extract from under the seats.

This was even worse than losing part of her bathing suit. She could always swim in jogging shorts, but the skiff was useless without oars, and she had no idea where to find new ones.

As she and Ian peered off across the water toward where the boat had overturned, Alice noticed something moving in the high grass at the far end of the lake's western shore. As she squinted, what had seemed a tall, weathered tree stump suddenly morphed into a stocky, gray-haired man, half-crouched and looking right at her.

"Christ!" She grabbed Ian by the upper arms and pulled herself around behind him.

"What!" Ian tried to turn so that he could see her face.

"No!" She gripped his arms fiercely and kept him in front of her. "There's a fucking pervert over there."

"Hunh?"

"This fucking asshole, staring at me."

"Where?"

"Right over there!" She pointed, but by the time Ian looked, the man was gone.

"I don't see anyone."

"He was right there. He ran off into the woods. I saw him."

Ian looked again, then turned toward Alice with an expression halfway between skepticism and bemusement.

"This is so disgusting!" she said. "Fucking perverts in the woods!"

Increasingly bemused, Ian pulled his sopping tee shirt over the top of his head. "Here."

Alice wrapped the shirt around her waist and tied the sleeves at her hip. The shirt hung down below her knees, but still, most of one leg was exposed, and the drenched material clung to her pelvis and thigh like paint.

"Let's get out of here," she said.

They hauled the skiff out of the water and turned it over in high grass. Then, arms around each other's waists, they headed back in the direction of the house. The trail passed through a small grassy floodplain and up a low bluff before entering the woods. At the top of the bluff, Alice stopped and took one final look toward where the man had been standing.

"I don't see anything," said Ian.

"He was there. I saw him clearly. This pot-bellied old man—in chinos, a white tee shirt, with long gray hair combed straight back off his head." She didn't want to leave Ian the faintest room for doubt. "Disgusting," she concluded.

Ian laughed. "I don't see what's so disgusting!"

"You wouldn't!" She punched his rippling stomach.

"He's out taking a walk, sees this gorgeous, bare-assed naiad standing on the shore of a lake—who wouldn't stop and stare?"

"He's a pervert."

"It's not his fault you're so beautiful!" Ian smiled and patted her butt.

"No!" She yanked his hand back up to her waist. "That's the last thing on earth I feel like right now."

《》《》《》

That night they ate on the deck, ringing the table with citronella candles to keep the mosquitoes away. As the light faded, bats appeared, weaving jerky figure-eights in the gloaming. Gradually, the sky beyond Quiddagunk turned luminous teal, then navy blue, while the mountain itself became a looming velvet-black silhouette. White points of light appeared above its peak, and soon the sky filled with so many stars that Alice became dizzy and had to look away.

Ian was telling her about his mother's grief when his father, a dentist, took up with his twenty-four-year-old hygienist. "Everything I had taken for granted about my mother was just gone. You tell her a joke, and she'd just look at you like you were a Martian. One time I made her a birthday cake, but she wouldn't blow out the candles. She just sat there staring at it, like she didn't know what it was. I had to blow the candles out myself. That just really scared me—like my mother had been kidnapped and then replaced by this weird woman I didn't know. I was just eleven years old, but I felt like from then on it was my job to be happy for her, keep her going, always show her the bright side. And... well... It took me a long time to realize this wasn't something I could actually do."

Ian smiled at Alice, but his eyes were sad. She could see the individual candle flames flickering in them, and the wavering glow against his lean cheek and muscular neck. "Oh, babe," she said softly, kissing him.

He moaned and let his hand fall onto her bare thigh, just below the hem of her skirt.

"You're beautiful," he said.

"So are you." She laughed. It was a perfect moment—one of those moments she hoped never to forget.

She told him about her own parents, who seemed to have been kept together only by their shared love of television and alcohol. It had not been uncommon in her household for whole dinners to go by without her parents saying a single word to one another. "But after dinner," she said, "once they got drunk enough, that's when the insults would start to fly. My mother especially. The things she used to say to my father! She was always telling him—right in front of me!—about how guys would be flirting with her—the fathers of my friends!—and how she was too good for him. She'd

Love

mock him for the stains inside his underpants. And for like… *sex!* I mean really disgusting, intimate stuff! I used to go upstairs and put my fingers in my ears. But the truth is I don't believe anybody ever flirted with her—this dumpy old lady drunk!" Alice laughed. "I remember one night she was holding her drink in her left hand, so I said to her—'cause I saw that her watch was on her left wrist—I said, 'Mom, what time is it?' She turns her wrist over to look at her watch and dumps her whole drink into her lap. That was so *mean* of me! She's jumping all around the room, going, 'Oh! Oh! Oh!' and I couldn't stop laughing. I know that was mean, but… The thing is, I really hated my mother. For most of my childhood. Just hated her. I don't know how my father could stand her. Somehow he took it. It was like he could reach up inside his brain and turn off the part that noticed her. That's why he drank so much. And he'd just watch whatever was on television. Baseball especially. He was a maniac Yankees fan. He wore his baseball hat everywhere. In the shower, I bet. Probably even in bed."

Alice laughed again, but not really at what she was saying. The whole time she had been talking, Ian had been idly stroking the inside of her thigh and ever so slowly moving his fingers up to ever more sensitive elevations. She had been pretending not to notice, just as he had been pretending to be doing nothing in particular. But as she started to talk about her father's baseball fanaticism, Ian's fingers reached a place where they could no longer be ignored, so she laughed, leaned forward, and, smiling, spoke in a low voice: "You are *very* naughty."

Ian leaned forward too, his mouth so close to hers, she could feel his breath. But just as their lips were about to touch, there was a crash in the woods.

Alice turned her head to listen: breaking twigs and the rustle of dry leaves. Something heavy was moving through the trees ten or fifteen yards to the right of the deck.

"What do you think that is?" she said softly.

Ian had not budged; she could still feel his breath in the downy hairs on her cheek. "A bear?" he suggested.

"No, seriously."

Now he drew his head back. "I *am* serious. It's a bear."

There was another distinct rustle of leaves.

"Bears always sound like drunks staggering through the woods," Ian said.

"You don't think it could be that guy from the lake?"

"Your secret admirer?"

Alice was silent, listening.

Ian lowered his lips once again, but she put her hand on his chest. "No."

He said nothing, but she could tell from the set of his head that he was irritated.

"Seriously," he said at last. "It's just a bear."

"How do you know?"

"Because I know everything!" He was grinning, but only like a defiant child. "Anyway, even if it is your secret admirer…" He slipped his hand up under her shirt. "… I think we should just give him his money's worth." Once again he moved his lips toward hers, but she pushed him away and stood up.

"Stop it!" she said. "This is serious. The thought of that guy out there really creeps me out."

Ian fell back into his chair and lifted both hands palms-upward in disbelief. "Jee-sus!"

Alice picked up her plate and hurried inside the cabin.

After a few minutes Ian came in carrying a tray filled with clinking dishes and the smoking candles.

Alice turned to him, a waif-like sadness in her wide blue eyes. "I'm sorry."

He put down the tray and took her into his arms.

She squeezed him as hard as she could.

《》 《》 《》

They rose around two the following day, had a pancake breakfast, then decided to walk down past the lake to a rock ledge, from which there was normally a post-card view onto the gray roofs and white steeples of the village of Eikenville. The weather was mediocre—drizzle and fog—and they wouldn't be able to see much from the ledge. But they didn't know what else to do in the hour or so before Ian was to leave for Brooklyn.

The trail down from the cabin had grown slippery in the rain, and they had to hold each other's hand to keep their footing on slick roots, muddy inclines, and lichen-covered rocks. A mist hung over the lake, reducing the far shore to modulating smudges of pastel green, yellow, and brown. Crows yammered invisibly in the gray, and a bright lens of water dangled from the tip of every bent-over grass blade.

After the lake, the trail meandered along level ground for about a mile until it veered abruptly to the left and opened onto a stretch of weathered granite that seemed to end in a wall of gray. As they walked across the stone, the fog grew brighter and gained depth, but once they had reached the edge of the precipice, all they could see were mist-dimmed treetops directly below; everything farther out seemed to have been erased.

They had hardly spoken during their walk. Alice had been feeling a weight of sadness at the prospect of Ian's departure, and Ian had seemed lost in his own thoughts, barely responding to anything she said. They had not made love last night—and Alice had blamed herself with a particular ruefulness. Despite having pushed Ian away out on the deck, once they were in bed she could not stop thinking about how his fingers had moved up her thigh. She wanted to run her own fingers down his turned back; she wanted to murmur something filthy into his ear, but somehow she couldn't, and so had lain awake for much of the night.

As they stood on the ledge, looking off in the direction where the view ought to have been, Alice felt as if their silence were hardening around them, and that if they didn't find a way to start talking now, the silence would solidify into real alienation (their relationship was still new enough that she worried one bad day could ruin it). She gestured toward the fog and, after a quick, shy smile, spoke in the singsong voice of a tour guide: "And here we have the picturesque village of Eikenville, first settled in 1785. If you will turn your gaze to the far side of the Millfield River just beside the old stone bridge…" (she pointed down and to the right) "… you can see the wrought iron fence on which Phinneas McAllister was impaled in 1835, after falling from the roof of the Congregationalist church, which he was repairing. And, a little bit further on," (she pointed again) "that copse of beeches just across from the Exxon station is where Grandma Kettlebottom succumbed to apoplexy in 1878 and lay there for three days before she was found by a passing chimney sweep, who had noticed an odd smell…"

Surprised at how well her improvisation had come out, Alice grinned up at Ian. He kissed her on the nose, but did not meet her eye. Without a word, he turned and started down the trail toward the cabin.

«» «» «»

The drizzle intensified as they walked. Their hair was bedizened by hundreds of tiny, silver-white water beads. Each branch they brushed dappled their clothing with droplets, and, every now and then, tiny pools that had collected in flowers or cupped leaves would spill onto their shoulders and necks. Their fingers became wet, chilly, red. Their nipples tightened inside their tee shirts, and their sodden running shoes made squeegee noises with every step. Ian took Alice's hand as they crossed a rushing stream and didn't let go on the other side. Somehow, after that, it was no longer difficult to speak.

They talked about friends whom Ian planned to see for dinner during the week before his return to the cabin, and also about this new band he had tickets to see Thursday night. He didn't say who he was going with, however, and Alice didn't ask. Ian was trustworthy, she reminded herself. He loved her. There was nothing to worry about. She lived in dread of ever seeming "the jealous girlfriend."

As they passed along the low bluff, just above the lake, Ian touched her shoulder. "Look."

He was pointing at the skiff: still exactly as they had left it, belly-up in the high grass—except that now three of the four missing oars were resting on top of it.

"Whoa!" said Alice.

"They must have floated to shore. Somebody must have found them."

"Weird," she said.

Ian drew his breath to speak, but didn't say anything.

"I think it's creepy," she said.

"It's not creepy. Someone did you a favor. That's nice."

Now Alice was the one who didn't speak.

«» «» «»

Ian left. The sun rose yolk yellow Monday morning. By eight, plumes of gold-white mist were rising like volcanic exhalations all over the valley. Standing by the deck railing, Alice could feel the moisture against her cheeks. Her sinuses filled with the thin, sweet smell from the pines, and with the deeper, headier scent of heated earth and rot. By noon the mists and clouds had cleared, and the forest was baking under a glaring sun; the cicadas were making their ringing racket in every direction, and the birds were silent.

By two-thirty, even the shadiest recesses of the cabin were so hot that sweat was running down Alice's nose and neck, and she could no longer concentrate on her work. She changed into jogging shorts and her bikini top, and loaded up a hiking pack with a bottle of cold water, sun lotion, a

Love

book *(Anna Karenina)*, and her sunglasses. She sang as she descended the trail, her flip-flops keeping a pitter-patter time with the melody.

As she came out of the woods at the top of the bluff, she glanced at the skiff and saw that there were now *four* oars—in two pairs, neatly crossed—atop the overturned hull. Alice pressed her fingertips to her lips, troubled most of all by the aesthetic arrangement of the oars, which made them into a sort of gift, and implied a relationship.

"No," she said aloud, shaking her head. "Stop being so neurotic. He's doing you a favor. It's nice." She lifted the skiff and slid both sets of oars underneath.

«» «» «»

As she had done almost every afternoon for the last two weeks, Alice spread her towel over the entirety of the bed-sized dock, then smeared her face, shoulders, and arms with sun lotion—hesitated half an instant, then smeared the tops of her breasts as well. Tossing the tube of sun lotion onto her knapsack, she stood with her hands on her hips and pretended to be wholly absorbed in the beauty of the woods, the dark-shimmering lake, the pale, hot sky. She made contented noises; she smiled and turned her head left and right, looked up and down, but took particular care never to give the perimeter of the lake more than a cursory glance, especially at the far end of the western shore.

One of her favorite parts of her afternoons by the lake was lying on her towel, eyes closed, waiting for the sun to make her so hot she could leap, without trepidation, into the water. She would listen to the drum of passing dragonflies, to the lapping of the lake waves amid the cattails, and to the sawing croaks of bullfrogs. Her thoughts would wander ever further astray, becoming ever less rational and ever more infiltrated by dream-like imaginings. Finally, she would drift into a five-minute doze from which she would awake refreshed, sun-baked, and ready for her swim.

But this afternoon there were no dreams, no wandering of thoughts. She managed to keep her eyes closed, but her ears were alert to every sound that could be interpreted as a shoe raking through dry grass, or a foot-thump on hardened earth, or a cough, or a sneeze, as well as to what she could not help thinking of as looming silences. Finally, deciding that she'd already been hot enough when she came down the hill, she cast aside her sunglasses and flung herself from the end of the dock in a belly-smacking dive.

«» «» «»

Sometime after ten that night, Alice pushed herself away from the kitchen table and went out onto the deck. She'd been hunched over the computer for close to five hours. Her back was killing her; her brain was aching and dull. But also she felt weirdly restless. Her dissertation concerned the emergence of child abuse as a social problem in the late nineteenth century, and one of the reasons she had not completed a single draft, even after six years, was that the details of some of the cases she wrote about often left her frantic and depressed.

There was no moon out, nor any stars. All Alice could see beyond the deck railing was a dense blackness that seemed constantly to swirl and reassemble, without ever settling into a definite landscape. The heat of the day was still rising out of the valley, stirring faintly against her arms and cheeks, and within her sleeveless cotton nightie—the coolest item of clothing she owned.

Alice could not recall a night remotely as hot as this at the cabin. She had no fans, and the ventilation in the bedroom was terrible. Perhaps she could sleep in the front room, but even there the air was stagnant, steamy, and smelled of mice.

She went back inside and brought out her cell phone. When Ian didn't pick up, she felt so fiercely irritated; she nearly sent the phone sailing out into the roiling dark. She made a second trip inside and poured a shot of vodka into a plastic orange juice glass.

"That's better!" she said aloud, leaning against the railing once again, but was not entirely sure whether she had spoken only for her own benefit.

All night she'd been hearing noises in the woods: stirrings in the leaves, gentle tappings and, once, something like a grunt; animals, no doubt—birds, squirrels, maybe raccoons—but even so, she'd been unable to suppress a frightened gasp at every unexplained sound, or to stop her heart from pounding.

She went inside yet again and brought the vodka bottle onto the deck. After her third shot, she could feel beads of sweat trembling on her forehead and upper lip and she could smell the drips running down her ribs from her armpits.

What she would most have loved would have been to cool off with a midnight skinny-dip, but that, of course, was impossible; she didn't even dare use the outdoor shower—the only place to wash, apart from the kitchen sink.

Love

"This is so fucking stupid!" she said, looking down into her empty glass.

Just at that moment, she was startled by her ringtone. She'd left her phone on the kitchen table.

«» «» «»

The very first thing Ian said was, "Sorry I missed you, babe. My phone was dead and I didn't even know. It's on the charger right now."

This didn't actually make sense; Ian's phone had rung and rung when Alice called, but she let the inconsistency pass because she was so happy to hear his voice.

"Guess what," she said. "My secret admirer found the fourth oar!"

"Really?" said Ian. "Amazing!"

"I know!" she exclaimed. "I couldn't believe it."

"What luck!"

"Yeah." There was a brief silence when she thought of saying something about how uncomfortable the discovery had made her, but she chose not to.

Ian asked how her day had been. "Good," she said, and then she repeated, "Good." She told him about swimming in the lake—not mentioning her anxiety beforehand. She told him about coming across a "tiny meadow" of wild sorrel on her way back from the compost heap, and about how delicious the sorrel had tasted in her salad at dinner.

"And right now," she continued, "I'm out on the deck having a nightcap. It's so hot out here I've got practically nothing on."

Ian made a low, appreciative moan. "I wish I was there with you, babe," he said.

"Me too!" She squeezed her thighs together.

But when she asked Ian what he'd been up to, he was silent a moment. "Oh, you know," he said at last. "Nothing much… The usual."

She couldn't help asking, "You didn't see anybody… you know, like after work?"

"No way!" he laughed. "After all that not-sleeping you and I did over the weekend, I came right home and just passed out in front of the television. That's another reason I didn't hear your call."

Alice was puzzled that he should talk about not hearing her call, since his phone wouldn't have rung if the battery had been dead, but again she said nothing.

They talked a while about his work and about the friends he would be having dinner with the following night, and then Alice asked, as if she'd only just remembered, "You're going to that show on Thursday, right?"

"Yeah, man. Can't wait."

"But who're—I mean, you're not just going by yourself?"

"Oh, no. I'll—you know, friends."

Alice drew her breath to speak, but couldn't get her words out.

"There's this guy at work," Ian said. "Doug… I told you about Doug, right? Copy editor?"

Alice had never heard of Doug, but said nothing.

"His sister's going out with the bassist," Ian continued. "She got us the tickets. Actually, we're going to be on the guest list!"

"Sweet."

«» «» «»

After Ian hung up, Alice remained on the deck, looking out into the blackness, turning her cellphone over and over. Then, not twenty feet below where she was leaning, she heard a distinct, sharp crack—like the splitting of a nut, or the sound of one rounded stone striking another.

She went back inside and latched the deck door behind her.

Her father had a row of hunting and fish-cleaning knives in a wooden rack over the sink. She took the longest and most lethal-looking and put it on the table beside her bed.

Her night was one long collage of anxious dreams and feverish revelations entirely uninterrupted by sleep. Only when the ashen light of approaching dawn turned the leaves outside her window the color of cooked liver did she fall briefly into a restorative oblivion.

«» «» «»

The heat had not relented the following morning and Alice couldn't write—her sentences meandering, vague, and probably false. She gave up at around eleven, packed a picnic lunch and a big bottle of water and headed down through the woods.

She was too tired to swim across the lake—her normal routine—so, between bouts of reading and napping, she just paddled in the vicinity of the dock, mostly on her back, watching the clouds drift and mutate, and the swallows snatch mosquitoes out of the air.

Around five, the leaves on the treetops began to flutter restlessly in turbulent breezes, and huge gray clouds coasted out of the west, over the mountain behind the cabin. The breezes never touched the bug-dimpled mirror of the lake, but once she had returned to the cabin, she could feel them blowing the hot, mouse-fragrant air out of the windows and doors.

She barbecued chicken sausages that had been on the verge of going bad and ate them on the deck with a romaine lettuce salad and a tall glass of seltzer. As the light faded, the breezes began to surge into powerful gusts that she could watch sweeping across the valley, bending the topmost branches of the trees and turning up the bright bottoms of leaves.

After dinner, she brought her computer out to the picnic table, but no sooner had she booted up than one huge raindrop struck her temple and another left a beaded, diagonal oval in the dust across her screen. She returned to the kitchen table and, amid the whispery patter of the rain, had absolutely no trouble knocking her morning's cumbersome sentences into sonorous sense.

Not long after dark, thunder began to rumble in the west, and every now and then the blunt, gray peak of Mount Quiddagunk would flash pink or ice blue. The gusts came so forcefully now that, instead of sweeping from one side of the valley to the other, they hit it all at once, hissing in the trees, and causing the house to creak, crack, and groan.

Alice had just decided to unplug her computer when everything went white and a slamming blast knocked her half out of her chair. Before she had even fully registered what had happened, the cabin and valley went white a second time, and the instantaneous thunderclap was so loud, her whole body reverberated with it. "Holy fuck!"

Finding herself on the floor, she yanked her computer's plug out of the surge protector and crouched a moment on her hands and knees, trying to determine if the sound she was hearing was rain or the crackle of a burning tree. Another blast sent her flat onto her belly. "Holy fucking shit!"

Did the cabin have a lightning rod? Would a lightning rod make a difference in a storm like this? Who the fuck knew? She had always heard that a car was the safest place to be in a thunderstorm, but to get to hers, she would have had to run down a steep and slippery path beneath hundreds of tall trees.

Another lightning bolt hit—not quite so near—and she began to laugh, which struck her as odd, even at the time. She had, perhaps, never been rendered so utterly powerless, insignificant, and so absolutely at the mercy of massive and relentless forces, and yet all she felt was happy and wildly alive.

The wind was roaring. Twigs and pinecones were skittering across the roof shingles, and the rain hit the windows like sand and tiny pebbles.

Alice poured herself a vodka, and stood in the deck doorway, savoring the pinpoint chilliness of the wind-whipped rain against her cheeks, arms, and knees. But when a bolt of lightning set every single hair on her body upright, she retreated from the door and poured herself another drink. Replenished vodka in hand and sitting on what had once been her child-hood bed but that now, with the addition of a pair of foam-rubber cushions, served as a couch, she flipped open her phone intending to call Ian. No service—maybe a transmission tower had been hit. Nothing to do but wait and watch the sky flash lavender and pink and blue.

Soon the worst of the storm had moved beyond Mount Quiddagunk. Alice poured herself one more vodka and went over to the dusty boom box at the end of the kitchen counter. The boom box had once belonged to her, but she hadn't seen it in years. Her father must have brought it up to the cabin—along with a carton of her old cassettes—after she went to college. She put on a tape of eighties music that had been given to her by her high school boyfriend, cranked up the volume and, vodka glass in hand, started dancing around the cabin, pleased to discover that she could still sing all the words to every song. But mid-way through Billy Idol's "Rebel Yell," the music quit suddenly. There was a brief, brown flicker, and the lights went out.

The darkness was like a pressure on her eyes. All she could hear was the drumming rain on the roof, the water clattering in the gutters, and the fierce wind. Nothing to do but sleep. She felt her way along the walls to bed.

Some number of hours later, she was woken from a dreamless sleep by light streaming across her face. Billy Idol was crying out "more, more, more!"

«» «» «»

The air was so clear the following morning, Alice felt that she could make out each individual tree on the slopes of Mount Quiddagunk. Brilliant white clouds with slate-colored bottoms coasted through a deep blue sky. A faint, cool breeze streamed steadily through the cabin, allowing Alice to write with transcendent concentration until mid-af-ternoon, at which point the temperature had reached the mid-eight-ies—perfect for swimming.

She called Ian while she was eating dinner, but once again he didn't pick up. (Was this the day he was having dinner with their friends? She couldn't remember.) He returned her call just as she was getting ready for bed, so she went out onto the deck to talk to him wearing only her tee shirt and underpants. "There are so many stars out tonight!" she exclaimed, twisting in a circle with her head raised. "Zillions! I feel like I am standing on the edge of the whole universe!"

"Great!" Ian said distractedly. "I'm glad you're having a good time."

"So what's up?" Her voice was more subdued. "How're things?"

"Okay. You know. Fine."

"Did you see Maddie and Zach tonight?"

"Uh…" He was silent a long moment. "Yeah."

"How are they?"

They were fine too, and the dinner was also fine.

Alice was just beginning to become upset at Ian's strange monosyllabism when he told her that Maddie was pregnant.

"Oh my God!" Alice exclaimed, and they talked for a long while about Maddie and Zach's complex responses to the news. This was just the sort of conversation that might have evolved into another of their habitual rhapsodies on the cuteness of very small children, but instead they went on to talk about amniocentesis, deer ticks, disgusting omelets, and Zach's near bicycle accident.

Ian broke off the conversation. "I'm sorry I'm so out of it tonight."

"That's okay." Alice was glad to hear him acknowledge it.

"Mr. Soon" (the client from Korea) "hated our presentation. He didn't say anything when he was here. In fact, he seemed to love it. But then we got this unbelievably vicious e-mail from one of his underlings, accusing us of breach of contract and threatening to go to another company. Everybody's been sort of, you know, thrown for a loop."

Alice was about to make a sympathetic remark when she heard heavy footfalls in the undergrowth just below where she was standing and a repeated grunting noise.

"Alice?" Ian said.

She crouched and backed away from the railing, whispering tersely into her phone: "Jesus fucking Christ!"

"Alice?"

She continued whispering: "There's someone down there!"

"What?"

She heard another noise—like a foot being lowered carefully through weeds.

"Right in front of me," she said into her phone. "There's someone moving. I can hear him. Right below the deck."

"Alice? Alice? I can't hear you. You're breaking up."

She backed into the cabin and, crouching beside her old bed, spoke louder. "Ian, I'm afraid!"

"What's happening?" Now he understood. She could hear his concern.

"You remember that day? By the lake? The pervert?"

"Your secret admirer?"

She was about to say, "He's here," when she heard another heavy footfall, and another grunt. Without even thinking, Alice ran back onto the deck, shouting so loud her voice cracked: "Get the fuck away from me, you goddamn fucking asshole! Get the fuck away! You don't get out of here right this second, I'm gonna blow your fucking head off! I've got a gun! You hear me? I've got a gun."

Alice did not, in fact, have a gun. Her father never left his rifles at the cabin when he was not there. And, in the next instant, something about the emptiness of her threat and the hysterical tone in which she had uttered it made her afraid that she had imagined everything, that there was no one there at all.

"Alice? Alice?"

She'd let the phone fall from her ear. Ian's voice was tiny.

She snapped her phone shut. Listened.

Peepers down by the lake. A breeze passing over the treetops, making a sound like air easing through the teeth of a thousand people—nothing like the noises she had heard. She stilled her own breathing and cocked her head to one side, but even so: No footfalls. No grunts. No gasps. Just peepers and the breeze.

She went back through the cabin, flipping off all the lights so that she couldn't be seen. She picked up the knife from her bedside table and walked toward the deck.

Just as she stepped into the night air, her phone rang. "I'll call you back," she said, snapping the phone shut.

She crouched on the weathered cedar boards, phone in one hand, knife in the other, listening. She heard the long, pulsing hoot of an owl from the far side of the valley. The whispery flutter of a bat passing back and forth over her head. One tree groaning against another.

Peepers. Wind.

Love

She listened a full twenty minutes, but heard no sounds to indicate that anyone was waiting in the vicinity or making a hasty retreat through the woods.

«» «» «»

"You okay?" Ian asked as soon as he picked up.

Alice was back inside, the lights still off, all the doors latched, and her father's knife in her hand. "You're not allowed to laugh."

"What?"

"Don't laugh."

Ian started laughing.

"Ian, stop! I'm serious."

"I'm sorry." He was still laughing, but took a deep breath and seemed to get control of himself. "Really. I'm sorry. It's just..." He had to take another deep breath. "I don't know... I was just, you know, *nervous*. I was *worried* about you."

She told him about the noises. She told him what she had been afraid of. And she told him she wasn't sure anyone was there at all. She was trying to sound levelheaded and resolutely honest—the opposite of hysterical.

When she had finished, he said, "Maybe you should just come home."

"No!" At the mere suggestion she felt a plummeting sorrow. "I love it here. My work has been going so well."

Ian sighed heavily.

"You know," he said, "the whole time you were telling me about what you heard, I was thinking that it was probably a bear. Have you ever heard a bear walking through the woods?"

"You've already told me all this," she said impatiently.

"But wait a second." Ian seemed afraid she was going to hang up again. "You know how, when we were sitting on the deck, we kept throwing our fruit pits over the edge?"

Alice made a small, affirmative grunt.

"Have you been doing that on your own?"

"I don't know. Maybe."

"Well, anyhow, what's probably happening is the bear's coming up under the deck because he's sniffed out the fruit pits and wants to suck on them."

Ian sounded so confident of this opinion that Alice could hardly stand it. "It's late," she said. "I'm tired."

"So you've probably got nothing to worry about."

"Have fun with Doug," she said.

"Doug?"

"Doug. Your friend. Your friend with the sister." When Ian still didn't respond, she added, "The sister who knows the bassist."

"Oh," he said. And then he said, "Thanks."

As soon as she hung up, a voice sounded in her head: *he's going to the show with Gwendolyn.*

Gwendolyn was Ian's previous girlfriend. She'd dumped him about a month before Katinka's memorial service, and Alice had always worried that Ian was not really over her. Gwendolyn loved going to shows. The way Ian told it, that was the only thing he and she had in common. Alice, on the other hand, couldn't bear loud music. She hated how all the sounds blurred, and how, afterward, she'd feel as if she'd been beaten up. She'd gone to a couple of shows with Ian, but only under duress, and had stuffed her ears with toilet paper both times.

«» «» «»

The following morning Alice tried to write about how the nascent labor movement of the late nineteenth century contributed to the new and increasingly influential vision of children as vulnerable, incompetent, and in need of protection, but all she seemed able to do was load the page with disconnected facts. To clear her head, she decided to take her swim early, before lunch.

She noticed the phlox without being fully aware that she had noticed them, and so did a double take. Yes, there they were, on top of the overturned skiff: a bouquet of some dozen white and purple flowers, held together by a bow made from a long cattail leaf.

Her first thought was: Now Ian will have to admit I'm right. Her second was that she had to get out of there as fast as she could. And her third was that she was damned if she was going to let some perverted old man drive her away from a place she loved. Anyway, she told herself, if the old man had harbored ill intentions, he would have done something already. All he had done, in fact, was make kind gestures. He was harmless; she had nothing to fear.

Standing on the dock, she noticed white and purple phlox growing amidst the weeds and grass all along the western shore, with one of the denser clusters being exactly where she had spotted the gray-haired man. She kicked off her flip-flops, dropped her backpack onto the splintery wood, and then, not bothering even to take out her towel, flung herself into the water.

The cold trilled along her face and ribs, momentarily making it hard to breathe. But within seconds, she felt no colder than she normally did while swimming. Why had she never done this before? The shock was good. It had invigorated her and had gotten her off to a more rapid start. What a coward she had been! That was over. Never again.

For a while she actually managed to lose herself in the sensuality of swimming: the gurgling beside her ears, the eddies along her belly and hips, the spiraling bubbles trailing her celery-pale fingers as they swung through an evergreen obscurity. But then she began to think again about the phlox.

Once picked, wild phlox go dull and limp very quickly. The flowers on the skiff had been bright and springy, clearly picked only minutes before she came upon them. Perhaps this had been mere coincidence, but even so, it meant that the old man—or whomever—was quite likely to have still been nearby when she dove into the lake, and so could well be watching her this very minute. If, on the other hand, he had been spying on her at the cabin, and had raced ahead to pick and prepare his gift—well, then there was no question that he was watching her now.

She became caught by contradictory impulses: on the one hand, she wanted to drive all thought of the old man from her head, on the other she wanted to demonstrate, through the grace and efficiency of her stroke, her complete indifference to him. But the longer she swam, the more rigid and inefficient her stroke became. She felt herself veering to the right, and constantly had to lift her head to correct her course. Then one time she lifted her head and inhaled a dollop of water, which set her gasping and goose-honking for long minutes at the center of the lake. So ridiculous! she told herself. So absolutely stupid! She refused to even glance at the shore.

Once she had resumed swimming, she found that her stroke had gone jittery, and that she was weaker than normal. Several times she wondered if she shouldn't just turn back, but every time she shamed herself into continuing by thinking of Ian, who was never intimidated, never down—happy-go-lucky, always.

In the middle of the night, she had remembered a conversation with Ian the morning of her departure from the city. They had been discussing a friend who was trying to decide on a course of treatment for her breast cancer, and Ian mentioned that Gwendolyn's older sister had just had a mastectomy. Preoccupied by their friend's dilemma, Alice hadn't fully paid attention to what Ian had said. But in the middle of the night, she realized that he could only have known about the mastectomy if he was back in touch with Gwendolyn. This revelation had been promptly followed by many others, most coming in the form of questions: Could it only have been coincidence that Ian should reconnect with his old girlfriend just as Alice was leaving for two months? Had he really been kept in the city by work that first weekend? Was there really a Mr. Soon? (How could anyone have such a preposterous name?) And what about Ian's distraction the afternoon he left the cabin? And on the telephone?

The questions had just kept on coming, eating up her sleep. And, as they recycled though her mind on the lake, they did nothing to improve her swimming. The worst was that, no matter how hard she tried to abide by her normal rhythm of one breath for every three strokes, she never felt she was getting enough air. She started breathing every second stroke, and then for several strokes in a row—but always her lungs felt tight, unable to fully expand. Could the water she had inhaled be blocking some vital air passage? Were some of her alveoli flooded? She knew full well that, were either possibility true, she would still be coughing—but, even so, she couldn't dismiss them from her mind.

Finally she decided to give up and just head back to the dock. A nap and lunch—that was what she needed. She would swim later, maybe. But no sooner had she reversed direction than she was stopped mid-stroke by the image of the old man looking down at her as she swam up to the dock. She saw him with startling clarity, as if in a magnifying mirror: His tobacco stained teeth, partially eaten away. His eyes exactly the gray of his hair, but with pupils so tiny he looked blind. His leathery, brown cheeks bristling with white whiskers. He was smiling. He held out his hand to her. He wheezed.

This image so horrified Alice that she reversed yet again and swam toward the far shore as fast as she could, her arms chopping and her legs kicking so hard that the fronts of her thighs became knotted with pain.

For a while this seemed exactly the right thing to do. Swimming the length of the lake would be a triumph over fear and help restore her confidence. But she was too tired to keep up her fierce stroke for long, and once she slowed, she became aware that every time her right arm descended through the water she would feel a rightward rolling inside her head. After a while, she began to suspect that she actually was rolling in the water, and tried to keep herself steady. But then she discovered that, with the spinning inside her head, she couldn't tell precisely which direction was up and which down, and so had no way of knowing if she was steady or not.

When, at last, the rolling got so bad that she felt as if she were spiraling through the water, she stopped and lifted her head into the air—which only had the effect of transferring the spiraling to the outside world. The trees, the sky, Mount Quiddagunk, the phlox-festooned shores—everything she could see was rotating around her. It didn't matter how often she shook her head, or how rigidly she stared at any single point: the entire world was drifting, inexorably, from right to left.

All at once she understood what was happening: She was having an anxiety attack. She was hyperventilating. The hyperventilation had made her dizzy. And if she didn't stop hyperventilating, she would faint. In the middle of a lake. A hundred yards from shore. She would faint and she would drown.

Over the ensuing minutes, one tiny voice in Alice's mind repeated over and over: *None of this should be happening. You love this lake. You're an excellent swimmer. If you weren't so afraid, you'd have absolutely nothing to fear. How stupid! How unbelievably stupid!* But all the rest of her mind was given over to terror. She forgot how to swim. She thrashed. She screamed. She swallowed more than one mouthful of water and never felt she was getting enough air.

For what seemed hours, she thought she was making no progress whatsoever toward shore. But then, just when her lungs felt sucked shut from the vacuum inside them, and she thought she had no more strength in her arms, she realized that in only a few more strokes—four, six, ten—she would be close enough to the shore to lower her feet and stand.

And, indeed, seconds later, her feet settled into silky slime. And seconds after that, she staggered through the warm shallows and collapsed face-down onto cool, ticking grass—sobbing, breathless, shamed; so deeply, deeply shamed.

«» «» «»

She packed her clothes, her books, and her computer, and hauled her bags out onto the deck—only to bring them right back inside and unpack them.

All of the homecoming scenes that came into her mind were intolerable: She saw Ian's surprise gradually yielding to recognition of her flagrant and stupid cowardice. She saw how his tender consolations would do nothing to conceal his swelling pride at his manly capability. And then, because the earliest she could have arrived home would have been while Ian was at the rock concert, she imagined the apartment door flying open, and Ian and Gwendolyn tumbling in, mouth to mouth, their hands at each other's crotches. Worse, she saw herself watching the green digits on her bedside clock all through the long, grim night and into the first grays and pinks of what would surely be the most awful day of her life.

Why bring that on herself—any of it? All she had to do was endure one night and then Ian would be there; she could return home with him, if she still wanted to, and he would never have to know why.

One night!

She could do that—no, she *had* to do that! How could she live with herself if she gave in, yet again, to her fear? Her groundless, paranoid, stupid, stupid fear.

Once she had unpacked and put away her belongings, she decided to walk to the ledge where she had gone with Ian. She wanted to steady her nerves and just look out onto something beautiful. But when she arrived at the ledge, she was surprised that the view wasn't anywhere as picturesque as she had remembered it. Yes, there were a couple of steeples, but also three gas stations, a strip mall, and, along the river, a long, low nineteenth century factory with cinderblocked windows and a gaping hole in its roof, through which Alice could look down onto a charred floor and wall and a heap of garbage.

On the way back to the cabin, she felt a certain diminishment of tension between her temples and in her shoulders. Everything's getting better, she told herself. You're back in control. When she got to the skiff, she grabbed the now wilted phlox, ripped off their cattail-leaf bow, and scattered them across the path.

«» «» «»

As the western flanks of Mount Quiddagunk went gold and orange, Alice barbecued an elaborate dinner of chicken with an oregano sauce and yellow squash, pausing frequently as she cooked, and then as she ate, to sip from or refill her juice glass of vodka.

"You can do this," she said aloud. "There's no reason why not."

But then the sun was down, and an ever-deepening gloom accumulated beneath the trees and diffused east to west across the sky. Soon everything would be black, and the space where Alice could feel at home would shrink to the quavering oblong illuminated by her citronella candles, and to the incandescently illuminated interior of the cabin. Her head throbbed;

her spirits sank ever lower—less at the prospect of the long, anxiety-filled night than at the fact of her anxiety itself. Stupid, stupid, stupid.

Finally she said aloud, "Fuck it! If you want to get out of here—just do it! Stop second-guessing yourself."

No sooner had these words left her lips than the whole night seemed brighter and more welcoming. Yes! The perfect decision! Why hadn't this come to her sooner? Why did she always deprive herself of what she wanted most?

There was, of course, the small matter of those half-dozen vodka shots, but she figured that by the time she had finished packing, rumbled her car down the rutted logging road and traversed the five-mile-long dirt road to the two-lane blacktop (the first place she was likely to encounter traffic), she would be fit enough to drive.

As it was already dark and she didn't want to travel the long uneven trail down to the car more than once, she only packed her computer and as many clothes as she could stuff into a single suitcase. She could come back for the rest of her things another time—maybe make a weekend of it with Ian.

«» «» «»

She was standing on the deck, looking down the steps into a pool of throbbing darkness. Her computer bag was slung over her shoulder; she gripped her suitcase with one hand and, with the other, a high-power, steel-cased flashlight, long and heavy enough to be used as a club. The loudest sound in the night was the pounding of her heart. Sweat trickled in front of her ears and into the hollow at the base of her neck. The metal of the flashlight grew slippery under her fingers.

"It's like jumping out of a tree," she told herself. "Just start, then it's over."

She flicked on the flashlight, and—suitcase against her hip—began to lumber sideways down the illuminated steps. Once she was actually moving through the woods, she felt a flutter of panic at the way the flashlight cloaked everything it did not directly illuminate in impenetrable blackness. But the trail was winding, steep, muddy, and crossed by myriad roots; without the flashlight she couldn't move.

"Fuck it," she said. "Just fuck it."

She got down the steepest incline without incident and began to feel that the worst was over. Soon she would be in her car, radio on, wind blowing in the open windows. But then she heard the snap of a stick over her right shoulder—although it was hard to be sure amid the raspy wheeze of the suitcase cloth against her leg and her own grunting and panting.

She stopped a second. Hearing nothing but ordinary nighttime rustlings, she resumed her journey. Just get to the car, she thought. Get to the car and go! But then, a few steps farther on, once again over her right shoulder, she heard, distinctly, the swish of a branch passing over something large.

Half out of a desire not to show her fear, half wanting to believe there was nothing to fear in the first place, she didn't alter her pace in the slightest, although sweat began to sting her eyes, and the hand holding the flashlight was trembling. She wished she could turn the beam off so that she wouldn't be marked so clearly amid the trees, but it was already too late; who—or whatever—was following her would know exactly where she was even in pitch dark.

The incline steepened once again, which meant that she was coming to the place where the trail made its final bend around to the logging road. Although it was hard to tell over all the noises she herself was making, she no longer heard any worrisome sounds behind her—no cracks, swishes, rustles, or grunts. You are so stupid! she scolded herself. You are so fucking paranoid!

Finally she was walking along the level stretch just before she would come out onto the logging road; she could even make out, flickering between the trees, the glint of her flashlight beam on the car's windows. But then, all at once, she came to a halt.

Perhaps she had noticed a slight movement or picked up some subtle sound, but all she felt was a sort of malevolent aura emanating from the blackness beyond the illuminated branches directly in front of her. Something was there, something big, overpowering. Her flashlight beam was quivering. There was a rushing in her ears. But she could not move. Her car was only yards away, but her feet had frozen to the earth. She was helpless. All she could do was wait.

《》 《》 《》

She had enough time to take a shower and put away her clothes before the apartment door opened and Ian entered alone.

"Hello," she said.

As Ian caught sight of her, he looked as if he had been punched in the stomach.

"I came back," she said. She was sitting at the kitchen counter in front of her open computer. She had been browsing Facebook without being able to take in anything she had read or seen.

"You okay?" said Ian, putting his briefcase down by the door. His face was glossy. He had been sweating, and seemed to be having trouble seeing her—drunk, maybe, or just tired. He had come home just exactly when he would have had he left right after the show.

"How was it?" she asked.

"Okay," he answered, but not as if he had actually heard her question. "Fine," he said.

He crossed the room and took hold of her hand, which she had extended to him. He didn't kiss her, only looked at her in a sort of stunned incomprehension.

"Things just got-" She had intended to say, "pretty weird up there," but her vision went blurry and she began to sob. Ian pulled her into his arms and pressed her head against his chest. "It's okay, sweet babe; it's okay."

Ian's words, his smell, the feel of his hard chest and strong arms released something in Alice, and allowed her an almost delirious sense of well being. It was good that she had come home. And being in Ian's arms was good too. He was a good man: tender and strong. And she loved him. How could she have ever doubted that she loved him? She loved him more than she had ever loved anyone in her life.

«» «» «»

Alice was lying in bed looking up at the multiple parallelograms of street glow on the ceiling, listening to the long, low whisper of Ian's sleep-breathing. For hours she had been flipping from side to back to belly to side, waiting for sleep, glancing every now then at the brilliant green digits of her clock, hoping to discover that an hour had passed since her last glance, but finding, always, that it had been two minutes, three minutes, eight minutes.

But then she was back in the woods, yards from her car, at the moment of her utterly pointless panic. Only this time, she could see that there was, in fact, a darkness moving within the darkness behind the scrim of illuminated branches. It was a bear, in a sort of room—a kitchen. The bear was standing on its hind legs, like a man, with its shoulders hunched slightly, and its arms out, gunslinger-style, on either side of its body. And the bear was looking at her with an expression of profound irritation, as if she had just done something contemptible, something for which she would never be forgiven. 🄴🄻

THE SLOUGH

Pasha Malla

I.

"I should probably tell you," she said, swallowing coffee. "I'm about to lose my skin."

"What? Is that an expression?"

"No, not an expression. People's skin cells rejuvenate every seven years. Usually it's gradual, but I've been using something to make it happen all in one go."

"What?" He put down his knife and fork. There was something suddenly disquieting about the idea of bacon. "How does this work? What do you use?"

"It's a topical cream," she said.

"Topical? Do you mean like up-to-date? Current?"

"What are you talking about?"

"No, but this cream—where do you get it? Do other people do this?"

Her arms, those two pink Ls that began at the sleeves of her tee shirt and ended clutching cutlery on the tabletop, seemed normal enough: not peeling, not cracking, not even dry. "I got it at a specialty store. It's–"

"Is this going to happen like a snake? Like you'll just drop your skin and then it'll be sitting there in the shape of you?"

"I can't believe you're making a big deal of this. It was going to happen anyway."

"Right, so why not make a goddamn spectacle of it? Jesus." The lump of scrambled eggs on his plate was a jaundiced brain. The bacon looked just like strips of pig, sliced off and then fried in their own sizzling fat. "When is this going to happen?

"When?" She shrugged and took a bite of her toast. He waited, watching her jaw work. Nothing flaked away from her chin or cheeks; no skin snowed down onto her empty plate. She stared back at him. "Any day now."

"Like, maybe tomorrow?"

"Like, maybe today."

«» «» «»

He had felt, lately, that his life had become a raisin—if only he'd gotten to it sooner, when it was ripe from the vine and bursting with juice!

But, no, it had shriveled. If he handed out his life to trick-or-treaters at Halloween, a retributive bag of feces would appear flaming on his doorstep. Or maybe someone would pee onto his mail.

She, on the other hand, was always up to something new. For the past few months she had been working toward a distance education Master's in film something, film and feminism. So there were countless DVDs that needed viewing. After dinner they sat on the couch together to watch the next off the pile. It was a Hitchcock picture and after some business in a hotel the action moved to a train.

"Oh, I know this one," he said.

"No you don't," she said, putting on her glasses, getting her notebook ready. "Hush."

"No, I do—it's the one where the one guy kills the other guy's wife or something, and the other guy has to do it too. Kill the first guy's wife, I mean."

"That's *Strangers on a Train*. And you only know it from that Danny DeVito movie."

"Possibly."

"This is different. It's about a woman who goes missing. She's a spy."

"Oh, right," he said, and within minutes was asleep. The dream he had involved Alfred Hitchcock and something about a riding crop, and snakes, everywhere, shedding skin after skin. He had to fight his way through the papery wisps of them hanging like streamers in the air. Was she in it? Maybe. Or maybe he was trying to find her.

When he woke it was to a puddle of drool against his cheek and her undressing.

"What's going on?" He sat up and wiped his face on his shoulder.

"The movie's over. I'm going to take a shower."

"No, not with the movie—with you, with this skin business? What is this about?"

"You're still on about that?" She sighed, standing there in her underwear: the pink of her body banded twice in white cotton. And then she disappeared down the hall and the lock on the bathroom door went *click* and the shower went *whoosh* and he was left alone with what was on the only channel they got on their broke-dick TV: figure skating.

"Why?" he yelled at the bathroom door, the shower hissing back at him. "Why?!"

What was the reason they had moved in together? He couldn't remember. Peer pressure, maybe, from married and responsible friends. Or mutual coercion. Or Catholic guilt, although they weren't Catholic.

At any rate, here they were, and there shouldn't be secrets, not in relationships—wasn't that a basic tenet, like not poisoning one another's smoothies and alternating turns cleaning the oven? What had she been getting up to in the bathroom? In the mornings something would happen in there and she would come out riding the gusts of an expensive smell. In the evenings the shower would come on and fifteen minutes later she would emerge towel-turbaned and otherwise naked. But now there was this business with the cream and the shedding skin—not the life he had signed up for. They'd engaged in talk of "some space," sure, but he also felt a right to know, after seven years together, *what was going on.*

The following night she disappeared into the shower while he sat watching figure skating again. Twenty minutes later here she came, a rosy fakir, all loofahed and nude and clean with steam billowing behind her. She sat on his feet and got out a bruise-colored nail polish, while on the TV the figure skaters ice-danced and he waited for one of them to fall. He looked down at her feet, up her legs, her stomach and breasts, all the way to her face. From head to toe her skin glowed in one taut, moisturized, perfect piece. Back on the TV, a fellow in a sequined pantsuit was spinning an equine-looking woman by the legs, round and round, to "Devil in a Blue Dress."

"Come on, fall," he said, slapping the coffee table. "Fall, you fuckers. Fall, fall, fall!"

One by one her toenails went purple. By the time they were dry the skating program was over. Someone had won: there were flowers and a microphone thrust at the winners' weird smiles. He switched the TV off, and unspeaking, they clasped hands and stood and went to the bedroom and had sex there, on the bed. He stationed himself between her legs and she said, "Plow me, baby!" and he said, "Okay," and plowed her for all he was worth.

But the plowing seemed mechanical. They were doing the right things and making the right noises, but there used to be a time when she'd flip him over and grind away on top and they would come together like champions. Now, not so much: she lay there with her knees in the air and when he finished it was onto her belly with a gasp. She patted his back, twice, and he rolled off and she rolled away, wiping his sperm from her body with a tee shirt.

They lay there side-by-side in the dark until her breathing slackened and he knew she was asleep. He began sweeping the sheets for flakes of her. Nothing, not even that improbable bed-sand he had experienced with previous lovers, way back when. But who was to say that he wouldn't wake to a husk of a woman beside him, the new version off in the kitchen crafting a morning latte?

He reached over and ran his hand along her thigh, up her stomach, her breasts, shoulders, neck, face, the skin smooth all the way. He felt for a rift from which the whole thing might be beginning to peel away, like cling-wrap from a ham. He would smooth down the loose edge, tuck her back into herself, and there would be no more talk of new anything and that would be that. But there was nothing; she was seamless. Casually, his hand drifted to her crotch, to the soft frizz of her down there. Her chest rose and fell, steady as waves. He lay his palm like so and eased a finger in, just to see: things were damp inside, and warm.

«» «» «»

"What I want is a record. A document."

Finally, they were getting somewhere. "Explain," he said.

"Think of all you've done in the last seven years."

He thought for a while, and then stopped, because it was depressing. "Okay not *you*, specifically, but... anyone. People."

"You."

"Me, sure."

"I would think of all you've done in the past seven years, but it would involve that yoga instructor who was on the scene for the first few months when we started going around together—before you ditched him, thank Christ—and that makes me sad for you. It makes me want to take you in my arms and kiss you." He shuffled his chair over, leaning toward her, puckering his lips. "Very quickly, and very hard."

She pushed him away. "Shut up. Seven years of your life, just flaking away, gone. This year I'll have all of them, my whole body, in one piece."

"And then what? You'll just keep it around? Are you going to press it like a dried flower or something, make a giant bookmark?"

"I don't *know*. It might not even work like that. I just..."

"The thing I don't get is why you'd tell me this now. You've been doing these cream treatments for how long?"

"I got it just before we met. I started pretty much right around our first date."

"Oh god."

"You should be happy! It's like I knew all along that you'd be here for the end." She looked at her watch. "Man, I'm going to be late for work."

"If it happens there, will you bring the skin home? Or just pin it up in your cubicle with colored tacks?"

But she was already standing with half a waffle wagging from her mouth, and putting on her coat, and now the bike helmet, and removing the waffle to kiss him on the cheek, and out the door, and gone. Left with the buzz of the fridge and his half-eaten grapefruit, he registered what she had said: "For The End." What the hell did that mean?

He went to the bathroom and rooted around in the medicine cabinet for this magical cream, whatever it was. But she had for some reason transferred everything to generic plastic containers. Some of the creams inside were a mysterious robin's egg blue, others white, others just cream-colored, the color of cream. He unscrewed the lid of one and sniffed. And another. And another. They all smelled like her. Or like little fractions of her: coconut + aloe + pink, etc. He crowded all the open bottles together in the sink, took a towel, and ducked down and draped it over his head so it formed a sort of cave. With the towel trapping the aromas, he inhaled.

Close.

He was late for work. And then, perfect: the fucking subway stalled between stations. After what seemed like ages another train pulled up on the adjacent track and sat there too. He looked in through the lighted windows at the commuters: the frustration on their faces, all those briefcases on all those laps. His own briefcase, on his own lap, had been her idea. "You can't go to work with a plastic bag!" she'd told him one day. "But all I take is a sandwich," he'd said, to which she'd replied, "Well, take your sandwich to work like a man."

But then there was movement. His train was pulling forward. He watched the other train go by, the faces of the passengers sliding past, the lights of the windows fading until they were gone and nothing was left, just an empty track where the train had been. And that was when he realized that he hadn't moved at all. The other train had left.

His still sat in the dark of the tunnel, waiting for some signal so it could go.

He thought about this skin business, and about the sex they'd had the night before, purposeful and sterile. He admitted to himself: lately things had gone stale. Maybe something new was just what they needed—a new DVD player, sure, but even better, a new skin. And as the train creaked into motion he began to come around to the idea, and then he was excited, and he was checking and rechecking his cellphone for reception so he could tell her, and was doing this with such fervor that he missed his stop.

By now he was half an hour late for work, so he got out of the subway to call in and let them know—what, that his girlfriend had that morning had an emergency, making implied references to her private parts. That sort of thing worked every time. And then he would call her and say, "Yes, your new skin is just what our relationship needs!" But his phone wasn't working and now the battery was on its last blip of power, too.

He was in that part of town where sweaters made from Guatemalan llamas were sold in abundance and everyone smelled like hash. Making his way to street level, he heard music—a song he recognized but couldn't place, played soft and sad nearby.

At the top of the stairs sat a fat man playing the flute. Two CDs bearing the fat man's picture were propped against a yogurt container with a quarter and a penny in it. And now another loonie—*cling!*—and he made his way out, a dollar poorer, into the neighborhood, acting as though he had somewhere to go, a place where he was needed, someone to see, trying to find somewhere his dying cellphone would work.

A store to his left was selling bongs and bongos. Out front loitered the expected clientele, who eyed him as he slouched by with his briefcase, phone aloft like a compass.

Here was a retailer of used clothes with a rainbow of jeans pinned over the doorway. Here was a place called *THE ANARCHIST BOOK-STORE* with a sleeping cat in the window. Here was a Medical Clinic of some description, and here was—hello!—*Your one-stop shop for natural remedies*, and then there was some Chinese writing on a sign.

The door-chimes were wooden and knocked against one another like bones. A woman sat working the counter. "Hi!" she yelled, smiling.

"Hi," he said. "Do you sell a skin cream—"

"Skin creams, in the back!"

"Okay!"

"In the back!" She pointed past a rack of soaps that were flecked with what looked like dirt. "*In the back!*"

"Thank you!"

In the back were shampoos made from all sorts of improbable concoctions, remedies for ailments he didn't know could afflict human beings, things that were technically foods but you were meant to rub into your feet. And skin creams. A shelf stretched from the floor of the shop to the ceiling, full of skin creams. "Good Christ," he muttered.

"Need help?!" screamed the woman.

"No!" he screamed back. "Thanks!"

But, yes, he most certainly did. All of the containers were the same: a label featuring a bushel of herbs superimposed over an alpine scene, and the brand name, *Natür*. There was never any explanation of what anything was supposed to *do*—just a list of exotic plants meaningless to anyone except, he imagined, the sorts of people who hugged too long, always.

But then, right at the bottom, wedged into a corner of the shelf, there was one that was different: *Formula 7*, in a metal jar. He picked it up and was amazed by its weight—as though the container were filled with pennies. He had to put his briefcase down and hold it in two hands. The metal was cool.

At the counter, the woman working eyed him suspiciously when he placed the *Formula 7* in front of her. This time she didn't yell, but spoke in a hushed, crackling voice that spoke of Eastern wisdom, or laryngitis. "You know what that is?"

"I think so. Is it the cream that—"

She waved her hand. "Four hundred dollars."

"Oh," he said, and suddenly realized what song the fat man had been playing on his flute: "The End," by The Doors, whom he loathed.

«» «» «»

At work no one seemed to notice, or care, that he had been missing all morning. From the phone in the stockroom he called her at her office.

"Baby! I found it! The cream!"

"Oh, no. You didn't."

"Of course I didn't! It's four hundred dollars! But I'm excited. I think it's going to be good. It's going to be great."

"What were you doing out there, anyway? I thought you hated that part of town?"

He spoke in a whisper. "Has it started yet?"

"No. No, nothing. I don't think it'll happen at work."

"How do you know? Are there signs?"

"A woman knows these things."

Was she joking? Since when did she talk like that? Since when was she "a woman"? But, he realized, she was right. A woman knew things, all sorts of things. Didn't she? Probably.

«» «» «»

That night her homework was a Marilyn Monroe picture. He liked Marilyn Monroe—or her bosom, anyway, although he hadn't seen any of her movies.

"Oh, you'll know this one. That scene of her on the subway grate, with her skirt blowing up—'Isn't it delicious?' That's this one." "Isn't *what* delicious?"

She gave him a look. "Just put the movie on."

He did. She took up her notebook and sat there in her glasses tapping her teeth with a pen and occasionally jotting something down. After a few minutes, he fetched a notebook of his own, one with a fancy leather cover her mother had given him one Christmas and he'd never used.

If after the skin change she emerged a different person, he figured it would be useful to have a record of how she used to be. This he wanted to seem covert but mysterious, and kept eyeing her at the other end of the couch and saying, "Oh!" and then scribbling something down. But she was watching the movie and working and didn't ask what he was up to.

Stats were first: height, weight, hair color, birth date, and so forth. Then he moved into slightly more personal information. Her favorite food was tomato soup, she had lost her virginity at seventeen while watching *The Hunt for Red October*, her desert island disc was *Graceland*, and she could not abide the squeak of Styrofoam against Styrofoam or the thought, even abstractly, of eels.

And then he wrote this: *I like the way she scrunches her eyes up like a little kid when she eats something she doesn't like.* He wrote, *Sometimes she laughs too loud in public and I complain but really I find it amazing.* He added, *Sometimes I find her amazing.*

«» «» «»

Years ago, for their second Valentine's Day together, they decided to eat at separate restaurants—the idea being that loneliness would reinforce their love. It worked: he pushed his food around pathetically with an empty chair across the table, the over-attentiveness of his waiter a poor mask for pity. Later, he clutched her in bed with what could be described only as desperation. It had become a Valentine's Day tradition ever since.

He added this to his list the next night, while she screened something irreverent from France. It required a few pages and an expository style that at first seemed odd beside the point-form notes, but then he liked. Looking up: in the movie one of the characters said, "Je t'aime," to another character, and that character said it back—although there was something Parisian and disaffected about the exchange. The French! They were so mean and great.

Opening his notebook again, he added another little story. The third time they had sex he grunted, "I love you," when he was coming, and afterward they lay in awkward silence on opposite sides of his futon. "I love having sex with you," he whispered after a few minutes, trying to make it sound like something he'd just covered and was now reiterating, casually.

He was reminded then of this story: one night a few months later they were at a thing for one of their artist friends. Over the crowd of people in complicated shoes they locked eyes and she winked. Something in that wink sang through him, warm. He stumbled beaming (away from some guy detailing his process) across the room and planted one on her, as dumb and happy and slobbery as a puppy. They had pulled away, unspeaking, and for the first time in his life he could see in someone else's eyes exactly how he felt.

On the TV the woman was now wandering morosely around Paris; her lover was nowhere to be seen. Meanwhile, at the far end of the couch, she was making notes.

He kicked her.

"Ow," she said. "Don't."

"Hey," he said, nudging her with his foot.

"Hush, will you? This is for school."

He nudged again and she looked at him, exasperated. "What?"

"I love you," he said.

She stared at him. "And?"

"And do you love me?"

"No, I hate you."

"Really?"

"Yes."

He looked at her. She gazed back, her expression impatient. He looked into those eyes, from one to the other across the beautiful nub of her perfect nose, searching for something. But he couldn't find it, because he wasn't sure exactly what he was supposed to be looking for.

«» «» «»

At noon the next day he went into the bathroom at work and locked himself in a stall. He put the lid of the toilet down, kept his pants up and sat. There was someone in the next stall over; he could hear the toilet paper being whisked from its dispenser, the scrub of it between ass-cheeks, a cough. He waited until the toilet flushed, the stall creaked open, the taps ran, the hand drier roared and the bathroom door closed. Left alone, he put his head in his hands and sat there like that, on the toilet lid in the stall in the bathroom, until his lunch break was over.

«» «» «»

He got home that night and she was still at work. The slick clock above the kitchen table, all chrome and Scandinavian, claimed it was half past six. She was usually home before him and had something happening, food or booze, when he walked in the door. In the fridge he found half a bottle of red wine; it had been there for weeks. He poured himself a glass and drank it, ice cold and sour, as he wandered around the apartment.

As he made his way from room to room, everything struck him as a relic: framed photos of a bike trip through the Maritimes, a table that had belonged to her grandparents, the fern that he had nearly killed and she had revived and now bloomed green and glorious in the living room—artifacts in a museum, a history of their life in things. What would it all mean when she came home with a different skin? Maybe they'd have to get new stuff.

He sat down at the kitchen table and from his briefcase removed the notebook. What had started as a simple inventory had become something else—notes for a story or a film treatment. Yes, a movie! One of those hipster indie rom-coms, maybe, something quirky starring a hot young actor as him and a hot young actress as her, with lots of talking to the camera and a badass soundtrack. Encouraged, he got out his pen to add another story.

One summer years ago they were shopping together, and the woman in front of them in line at the grocery store had a shocking sunburn—the sort that look as though the skin is still cooking, that it would be gooey to touch.

The woman was middle-aged, a typical July mom in a tanktop tucked into khaki shorts, a crotch that stretched impossibly from navel to knees. In certain places the sunburn—which spread across the mom's back, down her arms, up her neck—had begun to peel. White fractures split the red, the edges dry and ragged. They stood gawking at the sunburn while the mom placed eight boxes of ice cream onto the conveyor belt in a slow, pained way.

And then, before he could stop her, she was reaching out and taking hold of one of the flaps of dead skin on the mom's back and gently pulling it free. The mom watched the cashier ring her ice cream through, oblivious. He was horrified, but amazed. What sort of human being would do such a thing? And then something snapped and, before she could be caught with the evidence, she flicked the little ribbon of mom away.

On the subway ride home, groceries clustered in bags at their feet, he demanded: "Why?"

"I don't know—weren't you tempted to do it? It was just so…" She made a noise similar to those she produced during sex.

"No. No, it was absolutely not 'just so' anything. That was sociopathic behaviour. A cannibal might do something similar."

"Oh, come on. Cannibals eat people, not peel them."

"What do you think the first step is?"

"Please."

They would move in together two months later.

He sat there, reading the story over. It came floating up off the page with the milky miasma of a recalled dream. Crap. Had he made the whole thing up? There had been a sunburned lady once at the grocery store, he was sure—but had the peeling attack actually happened, or was it just something they discussed, or he imagined? He poured out the last drips of wine from the bottle, tipped back a sludgy mouthful, and closed the journal. He sat there for a long time with his hand on the cover before he looked up at the clock.

Ten past seven. She was late—very late. She'd never been this late before, not without calling or a plan. Maybe the skin had started to slough away at the office and she'd had to get her colleagues to help with the unwrapping. Or maybe something had gone wrong and she was lying on the floor of her cubicle, strangled to death by the crackling wisps of her old arms.

No, he thought: She was gone. She had shed her old self and life and taken off. Maybe later she would call him from some roadside hacienda in dustiest Mexico, all fresh-skinned and new. A person reborn, free of him and their life together. He imagined her riding her bike along the side of the highway, the skin peeling away from her body, flapping at her heels, as she made her way to somewhere better.

II.

Since Lee went in nearly three weeks ago, I spend my weekends watching movies with her in the ICU. She's got a list of classics she's always wanted to see, so on Friday evening after work I stop by the video shop between the airport and hospital and pick up the next three: *The Lady Vanishes*, *The Seven-Year Itch*, and *Cléo from 5 to 7*. We'll watch one a day and then I'll return them all on Monday.

Waiting for me in the hallway outside Lee's room is Dr. Cheung. "Hi Pasha!" she says, producing a hand to shake, which I shake. Her hand is cold. Her hands are always cold, and her voice is always alarmingly loud—especially for a hospital.

"How are things going?"

"She's doing well!" enthuses Dr. Cheung, beaming. Then she lowers her voice. "We've got the last of the scans back and think we can go ahead with the surgery either tomorrow or the next day."

"That's the Gamma knife thing?"

"Yes, we'll use it to remove the two remaining metastases from her brain. As I'm sure Dr. Persaud told you, melanoma responds so poorly to traditional radiation that we really think this is the best option."

"And it's safe?"

Dr. Cheung nods. "Absolutely. This, in fact has less potential for complications than the surgeries we did to remove the original tumors on her back. Lee has some literature. Why don't you go in and see her?"

"Isn't she sleeping now?" I step away from Lee's room. "Maybe I should wait?"

"No!" Dr. Cheung yells, her hand on my shoulder, urging me forward, voice cranked back up. "She's waiting to see you!"

I pause at the door. Dr. Cheung nods and gives me a shove into the room.

"Hey," Lee whispers. She's propped up in bed with a version of lunch on the tray in front of her: gravy-soaked brown mush, veggies, a lump of potato.

"Hey," I say. I put the newspaper, DVDs, and coffee on the tray, kiss her on the top of her bald head, and sit down.

«» «» «»

Lee's night nurse is Olivier, the quiet Congolese guy Lee really likes. If Dr. Cheung is a foghorn, Olivier is a thought. You barely know he is there; he whispers and nods and treats Lee with gentle reverence. Sometimes he mutters softly to her in French, "Ma petite puce," while he is changing her IV.

I sit watching for a bit and then Olivier turns to me and says, "Sir," which is his polite way of asking me to leave. At first I'd been offended by the nurses asking this—after so long together I've seen Lee in every state of compromise you could possibly imagine—but I've realized it's not about me.

"Ten minutes," Olivier whispers, and pulls the curtain around the bed, closing them off. I leave the room, then head down the hall, into the elevator, down four levels, and out of the hospital where I stand with the smokers, not smoking because I don't smoke.

«» «» «»

We've just started *The Seven Year-Itch*, headphones clamped over our ears, when Mauricio appears at the curtain, his sideburns two slick daggers on either side of his face.

"Knock, knock," he says.

Lee hits stop on the remote and swings the screen out of the way. "*Bienvenido*," she says.

Mauricio and Lee went to school together. I guess he tutored her in Spanish before she went to Mexico for a foreign exchange, then they met up down there and traveled around and he'd moved back to Buenos Aires. He moved back up here a few months ago, maybe because Lee got sick—I'm not sure. I'm not sure if they ever slept together, either. There's definitely something. I've always dealt with it by trying to seem okay with the guy, not asking too many questions.

"Hey, man, take my seat," I tell him, standing and offering the chair. "Please."

Mauricio's brought flowers, which he passes to me as we swap places. Shuffling the chair closer to the bed, he takes Lee's hand and runs his thumb over her knuckles.

"How you feeling?" he asks, staring into her eyes.

"Okay," she tells him. "Tired. The pain's not been too bad today."

"Yeah."

Watching Mauricio so close to her, I try to summon up some feeling of jealousy or resentment. But it's hard. My physical contact with Lee has become so perfunctory. Since the diagnosis we've had sex once—and that was six months ago and at Lee's urging, not mine. I capitulated but went about it as though she were something made of glass, the words *SKIN CANCER* rattling around in my brain the entire time. Afterward she went to get a drink of water and didn't come back to bed. Eventually, I went into the kitchen and found her sitting at the table in the dark.

Mauricio's stroking her arm now, up and down—an arm bruised and scarred from all the lines and IVs constantly being threaded into it. The bruises are purple and yellow blotches. The newest scars are red and wet; the oldest, black scabs. She looks like a junkie. Lee's arms make something sickly rise in my throat and a prickly feeling fizz from my feet to my head. They are nothing I'd want to touch.

But Mauricio doesn't seem to mind. He runs his fingers up and down her arms like the marks aren't even there. They gaze into one another's eyes. Her hair's been gone for ages, but since they stopped the chemo there's a downy sort of fuzz growing back. Mauricio cradles the back of her neck with his hand, then leans in to scoop her into his arms. He holds her, softly but firmly. She hugs him back. They're this way for a long time, while I stand in the corner of the room, cradling the bouquet of flowers like some sort of caddie or valet.

《》 《》 《》

When visiting hours are over Mauricio and I leave together.

"I'm going to meet some friends to go dancing," he says. "Do you want to come?"

"Dancing? No man, I'm probably good."

He sambas off into the night and I make my way to the subway station.

Riding home, slumped in my seat as the train roars and squeals its way between stops, I watch a couple at the end of the car making out. They are seventeen, maybe eighteen. Their jaws are really working. At one point the girl climbs up and mounts the guy's thigh and starts grinding into him with her hips. He licks her sloppily from neck to eyebrow, then pulls away, panting. They stare at one another for a bit, then he kisses her on the cheek and tells her, "God, I'm so fucking in love with you. It's fucking crazy."

"Holy fuck," she says, kissing him on the forehead, the cheek, the other cheek, the mouth, "me fucking too."

«» «» «»

At home I pour myself a glass of cold, sour wine from the refrigerator and take it with me as I move around the apartment. I take an inventory of the things that are technically Lee's—stuff she owned before we moved in together. I try to figure out what I would want to keep if she dies. This is what I settle on: the microwave, the coffee maker, the DVD player, the big soft towel we fought over every time it came out of the laundry. But then I realize that there's no "would"; there's no "if." The doctors have given Lee three months, tops. All these things are already mine.

«» «» «»

At 10:30 I go out to eat. Most nights I do. Lee was the cook. I'm decent with a barbecue, can fry up a burger if need be. But we live in a neighborhood with plenty of cheap food: Indian, Vietnamese, Mexican. It's late so I head to the burrito joint down the street. I order a beer and sit with it while the guy behind the counter shuffles around getting my food together. I drain the bottle when my order comes up, so I get another one and take it and my tray to sit down.

"Pasha?"

I look over. It's this girl Giselle I went to school with. Back then I had a girlfriend—not Lee, someone else I met through friends—and Giselle had a long-distance thing with someone she met online. We'd go out for drinks with people from class and every night would end with just us two left, sitting on stools at the bar together, faces inches apart. We'd stay to last call and have this weird, protracted goodbye before heading our separate ways. I came close to trying something a few times, but in the end never did.

"Hey," I say. It's been eight, nine years, but Giselle looks good. She was always pretty, but that was never why I was attracted to her. It was more the way she'd make you feel like you and her were the only people on the planet, those big brown eyes staring deep into yours. But right now she's with some guy in a puffy vest, possibly the internet boyfriend. I never met him.

"Come sit with us," she says, so I do, sliding my tray between theirs.

She introduces the guy she's with as Philipe, a friend of hers from high school—right away I can tell there's nothing between them. I suggest they grab a beer and stick around, making sure that it sounds like an invitation to him as much as to her. Giselle orders a Corona. Philipe doesn't get anything.

"How are things?" Giselle asks. "Still dating that teacher?"

"No, we broke up years ago," I say. She doesn't ask any more than that, so I don't offer anything. "What about you? How's your cyber-man?"

"Ha, right. Him. We broke up," she says, then adds, "too."

We drink. Philipe has found an *Auto Trader* that seems to have piqued his interest. I tell Giselle about how I work at the airport now, in the bookstore. "All my literary ambitions have at last been realized," I say, and she laughs.

Five minutes later I'm done eating and I've got two beers in me. With seven dollars worth of rice and beans my only meal of the day, I'm feeling both of them. "You guys want to go grab another drink?"

Philipe and his puffy vest can't. Giselle looks at him, then me. "I wouldn't mind, actually," she says, and turns back to her friend. "Can we catch up later?"

«» «» «»

At the pub down the street we both want the same beer, the house pale, so I order a pitcher. Giselle suggests we sit at the bar. "Like old times," she says. The bartender leans in with a candle and our jug and I pay him. Giselle pours and we sit there for a moment, watching the flame distort and refract through our pint glasses.

"Cheers," she says. "Good to see you."

We look one another in the eye as we drink, put the beers down and keep looking.

Our conversation flits between old stories from school and updates on classmates. Neither of us is doing much writing any more—although she's done slightly better, working as a copy editor at some trade magazine. We tell one another where we're living. I don't ask if she's got roommates, and she doesn't ask me. I never once need to lie about anything.

Then the pitcher's done.

"Want another?" she asks, giving the empty jug a wiggle. Her face is flushed. "It's on me."

It feels good to be out with someone. "Sure," I say, and pat her leg. "It's nice to see you."

"It's *great* to see you."

We drink, and soon we're drunk, and we're close, and there's a lot more touching: thighs, shoulders, elbows. She gets in so close that my knee slides between hers. Her eyes are heavy-lidded. By the time the third pitcher comes and we're both scrounging for change to pay for it my face feels like rubber and we're holding hands.

«» «» «»

"Isn't that what you were wearing yesterday?"

"This?" I wipe the sweat off my top lip with the back of my hand. "Yeah, laundry day, got a little desperate. Ran out of quarters."

"You reek," she says. "What'd you drink last night?"

Lee's really alert today, sitting up straight. There are days like this every now and then, when it's hard to believe how sick she is. She's her old sharp self, watching me shrewdly. I try to meet her eyes and hold them.

She looks out the window. It's been alternating rain and snow all morning. "I'm going in tomorrow morning for the Gamma knife surgery."

"Why do they call it a knife, anyway? It's not a *knife*, exactly, is it?"

"No, they—" She collapses, coughing. I spring up out of my chair to help her, but end up just sort of hovering while she hacks and retches. When it's over she picks her sentence up where she left it. "—do it with a laser sort of thing. You don't feel any pain or anything and you're usually back to normal within a day. If I was healthy enough I wouldn't even have to stay over. There's some literature there on the side table, give it a read if you're interested."

My cellphone rings as I pick up one of the pamphlets. It's Giselle. I hit *Silence* and pocket the phone. "Work," I say.

"On a Saturday?"

"Yeah, Sonya needs me to come in to cover someone's shift tomorrow. And she knows you're her. It's retarded. I should fucking quit."

"I'm 'her'? Who's her?"

"Here."

"You said her."

"No I didn't. *Here.*"

Lee waves the argument away. "You're not allowed cellphones in the hospital anyway."

"It's fine."

"It's not. It messes with the machinery."

"How?"

"I don't know, it just does."

I pick up the newspaper lying at the foot of her bed. She's done about half the crossword.

"Don't do any clues," she says. "I'm going to do it."

"I wasn't."

"Yeah, right. You always come in here and do them."

"Since when? I hate crossword puzzles."

"You're always doing them. You always come in here and wreck it."

She gets coughing again. I watch her and try to summon some inkling of compassion but I can't. All I feel is impatient. I think about waking up that morning in Giselle's bed feeling no guilt, just inconvenienced at having to come to the hospital. When Lee's done coughing I sit there saying nothing. I want to leave.

"Can you get me a coffee?" she says.

"Are you supposed to have coffee?"

"I always have coffee. Just get me one. And don't put cream in it this time, you always put too much in. Just bring me a creamer and let me do it."

I look at her for a minute: the bald head, the gaunt face, the wreck of a body. But in the eyes is something very much alive. It's anger—not anger at me, specifically; I just happen to be in its path. Lee's not supposed to have coffee, especially less than twenty-four hours before surgery. She knows it and she knows I know it. Her wanting one now is not about coffee. She's letting me know she's given up, she's letting go. She doesn't care anymore. And she wants me to be complicit in that.

So I get up and go get Lee a coffee.

«» «» «»

"You remember Buster?" I ask Giselle that evening on the phone.

"Oh, right—your parents' dog? You brought him around once. He was cute."

"Yeah, we had to put him down last year."

"Aw."

"He was about sixteen. By the end he got to the point where he was pissing himself, falling down the stairs. So after like six months of him getting worse and worse eventually my mom decided it was time to put the poor guy down—which was, you know, pretty sad. But I guess she let him into the backyard to take a shit before the appointment and he just went for it, bounding around like a puppy. Like, 'Hey, don't kill me, look, I'm still happy, I can have a good time!'"

I trail off then, trying to remember where this story came from or where it might lead. I'm just lying there on the couch, Lee's Gamma knife pamphlet unfolded on my chest. "But, you know," I say, "she took him in anyway. My mom's a heartless bitch like that."

Giselle laughs. "I never met your mom, I don't think."

"She'd like you," I say, and then actually wonder if she would. She never liked Lee.

Giselle's quiet. Then, "I want to see you," she says.

"Yeah. Me too."

"I'll come over."

I look around the apartment, at the tastefully framed art, the symmetrical placement of furniture, the knick-knacks. Even if I took the photos of Lee and her family down, it'd be obvious I didn't live here alone. This isn't a single guy's place. "That's okay. Let me come see you," I say.

"Okay."

"Should I come now?"

"Yeah, hurry," says Giselle, and I do.

«» «» «»

"I'll be by right after work, okay? It sucks I got called in."

"Hey, someone's got to bring home the bacon," Lee says. But then there's only breathing on the other end of the line, hollow and raspy. She doesn't say anything else.

I hang up the phone and Sonya's standing there staring at me. She's been managing the store since well before I started, a trundling garbage truck of a woman who thinks she's worldly because she works in an airport, despite never actually having been anywhere herself.

"How's Lee?" asks Sonya.

"Oh, you know. Same."

"Sorry, Pasha."

I try to make my face look however it's supposed to. "Thanks," I say.

It's been months since I worked a Sunday. I've forgotten how quiet the terminal gets. The few customers we get in are just trying to kill time before their flights, idly browsing the hardcover bestsellers, the racks, the Sudoku books, the travel guides, rarely buying anything. We carry this series of classics bound in fake leather that always draws interest (although few sales). They're classy-looking editions, but expensive, and printed on paper that reminds me of Bibles.

Burying my face in anything is more appealing than dealing with Sonya, so I join the browsers. After a quick pass down the magazine aisle, in the fiction section I've exhausted most of our selection (from Albom to Sheldon) when I notice one of those fake leather classics called *Adventures in the Skin Trade*. It's up on the top shelf and definitely not one I've seen before.

I reach up for it, but stop. My hand sort of hovers there over the spine while I imagine this skin trade business: people emerging from their outer casings, sloughing them off into rubbery piles at their feet, then donning new ones and heading out into the world. I don't take the book down. Back at the register, Sonya looks at me funny, but her face quickly folds into some puppy-eyed approximation of sympathy.

"You doing okay, bud?" she says, and wraps one of those flabby arms around my shoulder. A customer looks awkwardly up from the copy of *Time* he's reading, then back down at the page. Sonya's so close I can smell the cat odor on her. "Need a hug?" she says, and before I can respond, swallows me into one.

《》 《》 《》

"Who's Lee?"

Giselle and I have just gotten our food when this happens. It's like she pulled a severed head from underneath the table and dumped it onto my plate.

"Lee," I say. I don't know what is expected of me. I wait.

Except Giselle is waiting too.

"Lee is my girlfriend."

Across the table, Giselle sits staring at me with a clump of salad on the end of her fork. Elsewhere around the restaurant is the tinkle of silverware, the burble of conversation. But between us the air's gone silent and thick.

"She's sick. She's in the hospital." I glance around, then back at Giselle. "Last year she got melanoma. They've given her a few months to live. But you probably know this. Who told you?"

"I'm assuming *she* doesn't know about *me*. She'd be okay with you fucking other people?"

"It's… I don't know if it's okay. It's not okay. But we were done months before this happened." I realize that I need to seem more helpless. "I don't know what I'm supposed to be doing," I say, and look into Giselle's eyes in what I hope seems a pleading way.

I'm stunned when she shrugs. "Well, whatever. You're in a shitty spot for sure. But if you just need someone to be with, I get it. I just never thought I'd ever be 'the other woman'—should I feel honored or something?"

Apparently Giselle doesn't care for an answer. She picks through her salad for tomatoes, spears two on her fork, pops them in her mouth. I sit in silence, my food untouched in front of me, watching her eat. When the salad's gone she wipes her mouth with her napkin and flips her phone open.

"Shit, quarter to seven. I have to get going. I've got a date tomorrow night, but if you want to hook up later, text me. We're just going to an early movie."

She tries to chip in some money for the bill, but I wave it away. And then she's past me, out the door of the restaurant. Through the window I watch her on the sidewalk, flipping her phone open again, checking her messages, moving off down the street.

«» «» «»

After dinner I go for a walk in the park, down the path to the pond. It's busy there on Sundays, usually, but the evening is overcast and gloomy and there are only a few ambitious folks out, young couples pushing strollers or middle-aged women dragged around by dogs.

I sit on a bench overlooking the pond. There are ducks, a few geese, and a swan. Lee and I used to come for walks down here, back when there used to be two swans. I'm not sure what happened to the other one. No one seems to know. One day it was just gone. We used to joke that the other one had eaten it in a fit of jealous rage, vengeance for a big avian orgy with a couple of the ducks and a horned-up goose.

It was funny because the other birds are such idiots: the ducks flap quacking around and the geese hop about on the shore, pecking at the ground and scattering their bullet-shaped shit. The swan, meanwhile, just glides serenely over the surface of the water, neck like a question mark. A kid chucks a rock at it, shattering the reflection, although the swan looks unperturbed. I check my phone for messages. None.

Behind the swan the water fans out in a rippling V as it swims around and around. I watch it trace its graceful laps and think about taking that neck in my hands, the feathery cord of it, and just twisting. What would it feel like? I imagine the head flopping down, the vertebrae snapping, the swan crumpling and then sinking to the bottom of the pond.

«» «» «»

An hour later I'm standing in the hallway outside Lee's hospital room, listening to her and Mauricio talking. Olivier is in there too; I can hear him whispering. I picture the three of them, Lee and Mauricio huddled together, Olivier fixing lines and checking levels, soft and calm. I wonder for a moment if he lets Mauricio stay when he pulls the curtain. Maybe right now the three of them are back there behind it babbling at one another in foreign languages. But I don't poke my head into the room to check. I just listen.

My brain only registers the murmur of voices; if it *is* English they're speaking, the volume is too low to make out what's being said. Even so, I wait with a weird mix of dread and anticipation for my name, and at the mention of it for the tone of the conversation to shift from neutral and hushed to something else. But it never happens, and instead of going in I head back down the hall toward the elevators, their conversation fading behind me.

On the way down to the lobby I try to assure myself that Lee's doing fine after her surgery, that it was better not to bust up her little party. The pamphlet made it out to be such a minor thing. She's already back in her room, so she must be okay. But then, thinking this, imagining her lying up there in her hospital bed while I make my way healthily home to our apartment, I feel my stomach turn and the bile rise in my throat. I'm actually going to throw up.

Once the elevator reaches the ground floor I race to the bathroom,

The Slough

stumble into one of the stalls, and fall to my knees. But nothing comes up. I don't even heave, just gasp a little bit and catch my breath while my stomach settles back down. After a few minutes I lower the toilet lid and sit on it. And I'm like that, perched there on the toilet in the stall in the bathroom, when the announcement comes over the hospital PA that visiting hours are over.

«» «» «»

When I see Mauricio leaving the hospital my first thought isn't to follow him. Initially I just hope he doesn't see me, so I duck behind a pillar at the entrance and wait until he's gone past. But once he moves off I let him get about fifty feet ahead and then start trailing him—along the sidewalk, down into the subway, and back up in a part of town frequented mostly by white people with dreadlocks. Once we're at street level I lose him for a moment before I see him through a shop window buying something at the counter. I blow into my hands to warm them, watching from a distance. Then he's away again and I'm back on track, skulking through the shadows of the closed storefronts, off the main strip and down an alleyway lit only by the occasional motion sensor tocking on as he moves past.

At the door to his apartment, or what I assume is his apartment, he stops. I duck under the awning over a garage maybe six doors down. The street is otherwise empty. It's so quiet that I can hear the jangle of his keys and the grating sound of them sliding into the lock.

Before he moves inside, his voice comes singing through the silence. "You want to come in, or will you wait there until the shops open tomorrow morning?"

Taking my shoes off inside Mauricio's front door I don't give an excuse, just act like he's invited me over—and here I am. The place is immaculate, smelling vaguely of omelets. He doesn't say anything, just hangs his coat and pushes his way through saloon-style doors into the kitchen, whatever he's just bought in his hand.

"Do you want maté?" he asks. "It is like tea. I am making some."

"Sure," I say, and go sit down on the unfolded futon in the living room—which, I realize, is also his bedroom. The futon is his bed.

While Mauricio clanks around in the kitchen, I look around. Everywhere are musical instruments: guitars, a banjo, little hand-held drums, a keyboard propped in the corner. The only decoration on the walls is a watercolor painting tacked above the futon. Two m-shaped birds flap over a zigzag mountain range snowcapped in white; the perfect red half-circle of a setting sun washes the page in stripes: fuchsia, gold, crimson. It's a terrible painting, something the mother of a proud but untalented child might display only out of parental obligation.

After a while Mauricio emerges from the kitchen carrying a silver tray. On it is a clay teapot and a single, ornately designed, egg-shaped cup with a silver wand sticking out of it. Mauricio sits down cross-legged on the floor and places the tray on the coffee table between us. Without saying anything, he pours hot water slowly into the cup.

"Aren't you having any?" I ask him.

"Yes," he says, and then sits back. "We must let it brew."

A minute passes, maybe two. I watch the steam rise from the cup. Then he takes it in his hands. "At home we would have loose maté," he says. "Here are only teabags."

I watch as he takes a sip from the wand—it's apparently a straw. He sips, then sips again. I wonder if he's going to leave me any. I guess he sees my face, because he laughs. "You have never taken maté before," he says.

"No, I guess not."

"It is like a ceremony. I take the first cup to make sure it is okay for the guest. Maybe it is strange. But, you know. You are away from home and these things become important."

He fills the cup again with hot water and passes it to me. "Do you want sugar?"

I shake my head and put my lips on the straw. The taste is bitter and smoky—somewhere between green tea and eating a cigarette—but not unpleasant. I sip again. There's not much in the little egg-shaped cup, and soon I'm done. "Thanks," I say, placing the cup back on the tray. "This is the life, eh? Couple of dudes, sharing a pot of tea."

Mauricio's looking at me in a funny way. I avoid his eyes. He sighs, so long and heavy that it feels as though he's doing it for both of us, then fills the cup a second time and passes it to me, saying, "You did not come in to see her today." From his tone—not reproachful or accusatory, more restrained—it's obvious that he saw me at the hospital.

"Yeah, I was at work. I've got the day off tomorrow so I'll go by then."

"She thought you were coming. Everyone did."

I don't have an answer to that, so I twist to have a look at the painting above the futon, all m's and v's. When I turn back, his eyes are still trained on me like a pair of highbeams. "How did it go?" I ask. "Today, I mean. With the surgery."

"Good, she is doing fine." He gestures at the painting. "This was by my sister. She died in a car accident. I take it everywhere I go."

"Oh," I say. I take a sip from the metal straw. The taste is mellower now, more potable. "That's sad about your sister."

"Of course, she was very small, it is very sad. It has been four years but still I think of her every day. It is nice to have something of her with me, you know? Some memory. And I like to have a painting because I can think of her making it, putting herself into it. Art is the opposite of death because it is always alive. No?"

Jesus, is he really saying this? But, whatever, I nod. "Yeah, it sure is."

"And what about you?" he asks. "What will you do, after?"

"After what? After Lee's... gone?"

"Yes."

I think.

"I will go back to Argentina," he says, with an odd sort of decisiveness.

"You will?"

"Yes," he says, and nods. "Unless you need me here."

"Mauricio, just go home."

I catch myself and look over. Kneeling there on the other side of the coffee table, his mouth hangs half open as though he's about to say something. But then he closes it.

"I mean," I add, "you've already done so much. We're really grateful. But you must have your own life to get back to."

Mauricio just lies down, right there on the floor. He doesn't say anything.

I finish what's left in the cup, slurping up the last few drops a little too loudly. Then the room descends back into silence. Mauricio seems to be meditating, or sleeping, his eyes closed, body supine. Meanwhile— and maybe it's the maté –I'm feeling anxious and buzzy. I find myself having to consciously stop my feet from tapping.

After a while, I say, "Well, it's pretty late," and Mauricio jerks to his feet as though he's forgotten I'm there. He walks me to the door, holds it open for me as I make my way outside. With me standing in the street and him in his apartment, we shake hands, right over the doorstep. It becomes one of those extended shakes—just held there, unmoving—that feel like they're going to end with the other guy pulling you in for a hug. Mauricio's face is tired and drawn. I wonder if I look the same way.

"See you at the hospital," I say.

"Hopefully," he says, and lets go of my hand to close the door.

«» «» «»

Outside it's started raining. Just a light drizzle. I pull my hood up as I make my way back down Mauricio's alleyway, over a few blocks to the subway station to take a train home. Before I head underground, I check for messages on my phone. None.

Using the touchpad, I skip idly through the names, watching Giselle's materialize at the bottom of the screen and slide up, line by line, and then disappear. I stop on the one that says, *Lee (hospital)*. I call.

She answers quickly, her voice hoarse.

"Hey," I say. "It's me."

"Hey."

"How you feeling?"

"Tired. I was sort of sleeping." She coughs. "It's late."

"Sorry," I say. "I just wanted to know how the Gamma knife went."

"Tests back tomorrow."

"I'll call in sick and come in."

"It'll be early. Too early for you. Just go to work and come later." She coughs again.

"No, I want to come in the morning. What time do you get test results?"

"Fuck, Pasha, I don't know. Just come whenever you want."

"I'll come in the morning, okay? First thing."

"Sure, whenever you want."

"Okay." I pause. "Love you."

"Yeah," she says, and hangs up.

«» «» «»

At home I don't bother with the lights, just track mud through the house in the dark and plop down on the couch in the living room with my shoes on, hair wet. I sit there for a while, the streetlight outside filtering in through the window. On the TV's blank silver face is my own reflection, trapped and distorted somewhere inside the glass. The rain patters away on the roof.

Above the TV in a cabinet are Lee's DVDs, dozens of them in alphabetized stacks. Surrounding them on either side are shelves of our books. Wouldn't it be nice to write your life into one of those? To take everything and filter it into something charming and sweet, take your struggles and make them fun? You could reinvent yourself as someone hapless and amusing, someone whose missteps are enjoyable, not just wrong. Just slip out of who you are and repackage it all into something new.

I sit there for a few minutes, thinking in the dark.

After a while I get up from the couch and move down the hall, past the bathroom to our bedroom. I turn the closet light on, push my way through the clothes hanging on either side and, from way in the back, dig out a box. It's so stuffed full of junk that the cardboard is splitting up the sides. I pull out fistfuls of letters, cassette tapes, birthday cards, bills, postcards, receipts—here's one for a pizza delivered two years ago, in case we ever feel like returning it.

A few layers down I find an inch-thick stack of pictures, most of them self-taken of me and Lee, our grinning faces slightly skewed and off-center in each one. But I'm not browsing; I'm not interested in nostalgia. The photos I pile on the floor of the closet with everything else. What I'm looking for is very specific. I know it's in here; two Christmases ago I got the thing as a gift from Lee's mom and came home laughing. "What does she think I am, a twelve year-old girl?" I said, cramming it into the box. "Well, you know," Lee said. "Maybe she thought you'd get inspired."

Amidst a clutter of business cards and empty envelopes, I find it: the archetype of a journal, leather-bound and severe. Resisting the urge to blow dust from its cover, I leave everything on the floor and make my way with it back into the bedroom. There's a pen on the bedside table, a remnant of when Lee used to do her crossword puzzles before going to sleep. I sit down with it and the book on my bed, turn on the reading lamp, and sit there for a moment.

It isn't long before I figure out what to write. █

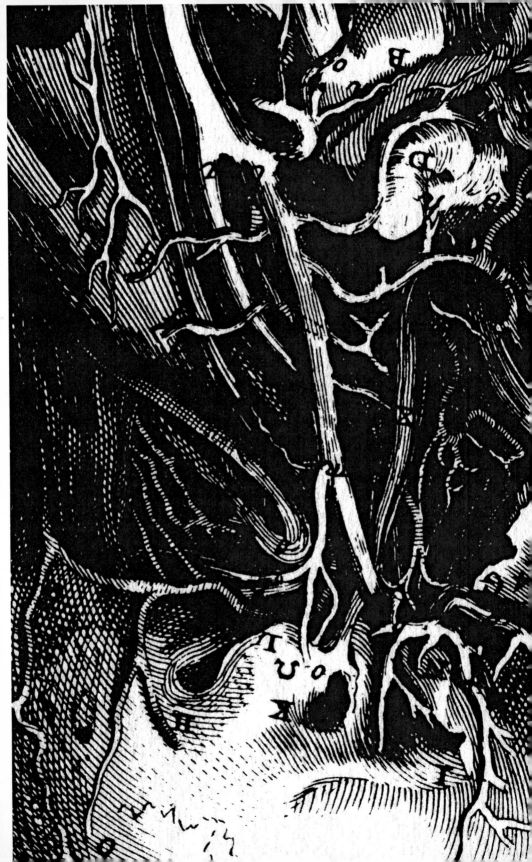

THREE GIRLS

Marisa Silver

Connie

Connie was always the first one awake in the mornings, and after dressing for school and making her bed, she went downstairs to the kitchen and poured out three bowls of Cheerios, sprinkling a bit of sugar over Paula's so that she wouldn't whine, her complaints threading themselves dangerously up the stairs. It had begun to snow the night before, and there was already an inch of the fine white powder on the windowsills. Jean came into the kitchen. She was seventeen and taller than most girls and some boys in the senior class. Connie had heard boys say that Jean had the breasts to make up for her awkward height. Paula came downstairs, and the three girls sat to eat. Only Paula had inherited the Nordic genes of their mother, her hair yellow-blond and straight, her face wide and pale. Connie and Jean were dark like their father, with deep-set eyes and the bruised circles below them that were impossible to erase with drug store cosmetics. Paula played a game of fishing single Cheerios out of her bowl with her spoon and watching them float in the moat of milk before eating them as if each were a treasure she'd brought up from the bottom of the ocean. Connie wondered at her younger sister's untroubled ability to commit so fully to every activity. As if you could eat a bowl of cereal or drink a glass of juice and that was all there was to it. When Connie finished her cereal, she waited until Paula had drunk the last of her sweet milk by lifting the bowl to her lips. Connie washed and dried the bowls, replacing them in the cupboard and the clean spoons in the silverware drawer. She liked when the kitchen was arranged so that you could not tell that anyone had been there.

Jean packed Paula's lunch and wiped the dribbles of milk from the table in front of Paula's place. "Pee and brush," she said to Paula.

"I already did," Paula said. She was seven years old.

"Let me smell," Jean said, leaning over her sister. She didn't need to sniff Paula's breath before Paula retreated to the downstairs bathroom.

"She just stands there, you know. At the sink," Connie said. "She doesn't brush."

"I know," Jean said. She slipped into her winter coat.

"Aren't you going to do anything about it?"

"Why should I?" Jean said as she walked outside. Connie watched through the window as Jean pulled the garbage cans down the drive to the curb. Connie filled Whisper's bowl with kibble. The old hound struggled up from where he was lying by the heating vent, moved lazily to inspect the situation, then lay down again. Jean came back inside with the cold air, her cheeks and hands already red. She refused to wear a hat and gloves, even on the coldest days of winter.

"He's not eating again," Connie said, staring at the dog. "He needs to go to the vet."

"You worry too much."

"No I don't."

"Yes you do. It's a drag."

Jean glanced towards the stairs, and Connie knew she was thinking about her parents. They would not want to be bothered with Whispers. "He'll eat when he's hungry enough."

Paula came out from the bathroom and Jean handed her the neon green parka that had been her own, and then Connie's. Connie remembered her mother saying she'd chosen the unlikely color so that she could always find her children, as though it were easy to lose them, but Connie thought her mother hadn't much cared what color the coat was, and that she had not thought about the fact that her children would be called "caterpillar" or "puke" when they wore the jacket.

The girls walked down their street in single file along the narrow path that had been cleared by others' footsteps. The snow was not deep enough for the plows yet. Drivers were being careful with speed, and the few other people making their way from their homes to their cars walked with careful steps. Connie had the impression that the world had become like an old person overnight, uncertain, wary of danger. They reached the elementary school and Paula ran towards the front door along with the other children. Connie tried to remember when she had run like that, just to get someplace a little faster.

All day long it snowed, and Connie watched out the window of each of her classrooms, paying little attention to the lessons. The relentlessness of the storm made the students impatient, and there was a kind of unfocussed excitement in the air. The bells ringing at the end of each period seemed louder and more disruptive than usual, and as the sky darkened, the brightly lit classrooms felt isolated, as if they were boxes of light floating in dark space. Anxiety slid beneath Connie's skin like a worm. She looked for Jean in the hallways during breaks, but she couldn't find her. Finally, a voice came over the PA system and announced that there would be an early dismissal due to the storm. Connie met up with Jean by the front door and together they made their way to Paula's school, heads bent low as if they were using them to break through the wall of snow the way explorers might use a machete to cut down tangled brush in a jungle. Connie thought that Jean must be regretting her choice of shoes over boots and her missing hat, but Connie didn't mention it. It was the kind of thing a mother would say, and Connie didn't want Jean to make fun of her.

«» «» «»

The family had attended the faculty Christmas party the night before. Connie's parents taught at the local college, and every year Connie's mother made them dress nicely and re-instructed them on how to shake hands and look people in the eye. Eggnog and decorated cookies and a plate of cheese and crackers were set out on the polished wood table in the President's house. Paula got caught up in a game near the Christmas tree with some of the younger children, and just when Connie was about to suggest to Jean that they go find a place to sit and wait out the party, Jean started talking to a man who had a graying beard and wore a sweater that had a snowflake design on it. Jean put her hand on the man's chest so that her palm covered one of the flakes and the man laughed. Connie thought the man was fat and disgusting, but Jean kept talking to him. Maybe Jean was trapped. Sometimes when Connie and Jean were at the mall and they ran into a group of seniors Jean didn't like, Jean would look at Connie, her eyes widening meaningfully, and Connie would make up something about being late for her piano lesson or having to do her homework so as to allow Jean to pull away gracefully. Jean would smile conspiratorially as they left the group and Connie wouldn't mind so much that the older girls were probably making fun of the fact that she was someone who actually cared how she did in school. Sensing Jean's distress at being cornered by the man with the terrible sweater, Connie started towards her. But when she was halfway across the room, she saw Jean trace her collarbone with her finger, then draw her hand down over her chest and onto her belly. The man's gaze followed along, as if tethered to Jean's hand by a leash. Embarrassed to be standing in the middle of the room for no reason, Connie made her way to the table and ate a cube of American cheese. Her mother stood at the far end, watching as a man poured a bottle of liquor into the punchbowl of eggnog. Connie's mother put her glass into the stream. The amber liquid splashed over both their hands and they laughed as Connie's mother licked her palm.

Across the room, the younger children were fighting about something, and Paula burst into tears. She ran to her mother and buried her face in her stomach. Her mother juggled her drink while patting Paula's heaving back, making a put upon expression that was meant to ally her with the other adults in the room rather than her daughter. The way she comforted Paula seemed to be part of the way she behaved at these parties—as though she were performing for an audience, her gestures over-animated and her laugh too sharp. Paula was milking her grief more than she should have, enjoying the scene as much as their mother, but it had always been simple for Paula to evince anger or frustration or joy. She did not seem to have that other Paula sitting on her shoulder, always telling her not to do and say the things she wanted to do and say.

Someone entered the room dressed as Santa and the smaller children took turns sitting on his lap. By this time, Paula had calmed down and she leaned into the big man's face telling him her list of gifts. Eventually, grown women sat on his lap and there was laughter and someone fed Santa a drink that dribbled down his synthetic beard. Connie's mother sat on Santa's lap and Santa dipped her back as if he was dancing with her. She was wearing a skirt and her legs fell open and Connie could see where her thighs pressed together. When she sat up, someone said "What did you ask for?" and Connie's mother said "I'm not telling!" and someone whistled.

Connie found Jean, who was still talking to the man in the sweater. "I think we should leave now," Connie said.

"This is my sister, who doesn't know how to have fun at a party," Jean said.

"Where's Paula? Did you see where she went?" Connie said. She looked around the room urgently. She knew they had to leave the party right away. She felt it inside her, the queasy sensation she got when she was riding the tilt-a-whirl at the county fair and her stomach went the opposite way from the rest of her. And then her mother and father's voices cut through the noise in the room and in her head, their voices biting and loud. Connie's mother's glass fell to the floor and shattered, shards winking in the spilled liquid like silverfish.

"Get the coats, Connie," Jean said.

Three Girls

On the way home, the girls rode in the back of the Oldsmobile pressed low in their seat by the weight of their parents' silence. Their mother's head fell back against the headrest, her mascara pooling at the corners of her eyes. Their father strained forward to see past the windshield, as if he were looking for ghosts.

«» «» «»

"You made it!" Connie's mother said when the girls walked through the door from school. "I was wondering how you girls were going to get home." She had pulled out jars from the pantry and stacked them on the kitchen table. There were olives and tomatoes and tubes of anchovy paste. There was Campbell's chicken noodle soup and artichoke hearts and tuna fish. There was peanut butter and apricot jam. "They closed the college," Connie's mother said. "They've closed the town." She set her glass down and the ice inside it popped. The house smelled like the inside of the glass—a customary odor of sweet, tangy decay that lived in the cushions of the furniture and the curtains. "Snow day!" she said, drawing Paula to her in a hug.

"At school, they said it was an emergency!" Paula said, happily.

They ate dinner at four o'clock. Jean retreated upstairs to her room and Paula was allowed to watch television due to the special nature of the day. Since Connie's father had fallen into a nap in his chair, Paula had to keep the volume low, so all afternoon and into the evening the house was filled with a low hum punctuated by the boings and pops of cartoons. Connie searched for things to occupy her. The house did not so much change over the years as accrue, like boulders covered with more and more layers of barnacles. Books lay on top of books, bills on top of bills. Sometimes, on a Saturday, or during the long summer months, her mother would have a burst of energy and decide to organize a closet or their tax files, but these efforts usually fell short, and a row of worn shoes would stand near the front door for many months, waiting to be taken to Goodwill, or stacks of papers would occupy one side of the dining room table, forcing the family to eat their meals squeezed in at the opposite end. Connie sat at the piano and played a few songs that she had memorized. She opened up the piano bench and pulled out old sheet music whose pages were brittle and chipped. Underneath the music for "Oranges and Lemons" lay a kindergarten drawing of a skeleton. She recognized her ungainly hand in the signature. She felt the same kind of wonder an archeologist might experience uncovering a thousand-year-old cup, awed by the evidence of life so fully lived, and then forgotten.

"I'm going outside," she said.

"It's cold out there, Con," her father said. He had woken and was idly watching the television with Paula.

"I just want to look around."

"You're going to freeze yourself to death," her mother said. She was lying on the couch, a pillow on her stomach, her glass and a book balanced on top of it.

Connie waited for someone to tell her she was not allowed to leave the house, but when no one did, she put on her coat and wrapped a scarf around her face.

She walked across the street and then climbed down the embankment towards the river. The sky was heavy and low. Ice had gathered at the edges of the water, but it was thin and it broke easily when Connie touched the surface with the toe of her boot. The water moved slowly in the direction of the current. Little white sailboats glided along where snow had adhered to a gathering of sticks and leaves. The wind was strong and it found its way into every small crevice of Connie's body that was not fully covered—the triangle at her neck where her zipper left off and her scarf began, the band of skin between her mittens and the cuffs of her jacket. The cold felt like small arrows piercing her, and she knew that she should go inside, but she didn't want to just yet. She slipped off a mitten and held her bare hand out and watched the snow accumulate on it, and then ate the snow, biting down on it so that it hardened between her back teeth before it turned to water. The air smelled sharp and clean and empty and she took it into her lungs until it stung.

«» «» «»

The doorbell rang after midnight. Connie was in her bed but not asleep. She was dressed in the next day's school clothes—a habit she'd adopted that made things easier in the mornings. She left her room and stood at the top of the stairs. Paula had fallen asleep on the couch, her head in her mother's lap.

"Don't open it, Claude," her mother said thickly as her father went to the door. "Could be anybody. A tramp or anybody. In this weather, too."

"Who's there?" her father called through the door. The muffled sound of a voice came across. "Who? I can't hear you." He was speaking too loudly and Paula woke up, making a distressed noise.

Three Girls

Connie's mother slid out from under Paula and stood just as her husband opened the door. A man in a red ski parka stood in the doorway holding a small child in his arms. In back of him stood a woman and two other children.

"We've gotten stuck. The car stalled out," the man said. He wore a skier's headband around his ears. "We were wondering if we could use your phone."

"You won't get help in this weather," Connie's father said. "They won't send out any tow trucks tonight."

"If you wouldn't mind, we'd just like to try."

"Let them in, Claude, for God's sake," Connie's mother said. Her hair was messy and her shirt was only halfway tucked into her skirt.

"So sorry to disturb you," the woman said when she had come inside. "We couldn't get any service on our cell. Oh no," she said, when she saw Paula sitting up on the couch. "We've woken your daughter." Her voice faltered as she said this, as if she was uncertain about Paula being on the living room couch. She looked up to see Connie, fully dressed, at the bottom of the stairs. She glanced around the room and at Connie's parents, and some knowledge passed over her expression.

The man put the little girl down. She was younger than Paula, maybe four or five. She stared into the room, stunned by exhaustion. The other children were girls as well, older than the little one, but not as old as Connie. Maybe they were nine and eleven, Connie thought, or ten and twelve. They had blond hair that showed below their hats. All three girls wore ski parkas and matching ski pants. They each had different colored hats topped with tassels, which Connie imagined would fly in the wind as they skied down the mountain. Their ski lift tickets were attached to the zippers like price tags. The girls looked tired and shy as they stood behind their mother.

"The phone? Could I?" the man said.

Connie's mother reached for the phone but it wasn't sitting in the cradle where it usually was. She turned this way and that, her hands on her hips. "Girls," she said, with prideful exasperation. "Always jabbering away to one boyfriend or another." Connie felt her face grow hot at her mother's lie. Her mother dug the cordless phone out from beneath two couch pillows and handed it to the man.

"You don't have to stand there," Connie's mother said to the woman.

"Oh, it's alright," the woman said. "We don't want to bother you anymore than we have."

"We don't charge for sitting," Connie's mother said.

The woman smiled. "Alright. Thank you. Girls?" The older ones seemed reluctant, but she put her hands on their backs and gently guided them over to the couch. Connie saw the woman look down before she sat, the way you did in the movie theater to make sure there was no popcorn or gum on your seat. The smallest girl climbed onto her mother's lap, while the older girls looked around the room, taking in the piles of papers on top of the piano, the old shoes standing in pairs along the wall, the carpet, which was darker in the places where people walked most often. Whispers got up from his dog bed and walked over to smell the new people. One of the girls put out her hand to pet him, but her mother reached out and stopped her.

The man made the call, his back turned to the room. "How long?" he was saying. "It can't be sooner than that?" He ended his call and turned to his wife. "I called for a cab to take us to the fire station. I guess people are collecting there. But they don't know how long it will take."

The wife stood, lifting the little girl onto her hip. The other girls stood with her. "Thank you," she said to Connie's mother. "Sorry to disturb you."

"You can't go back out there," Connie's mother said.

"We'll wait in the car," the man said.

"You'll freeze yourselves to death," Connie's mother said. Connie remembered her mother saying the same thing earlier that day when Connie wanted to leave the house. How her mother had allowed her to leave anyway.

"It's no problem. We'll just run the heater," the man said. "They'll be here in no time."

"For God's sake, you can wait right here," Connie's mother said.

"No," the woman said, a bit too loudly.

Connie's mother looked at the woman carefully. "Why would you want your girls to wait in a cold car when you can wait in a warm house? That's irrational."

"I guess you're right," the man said.

"Tom?" his wife said.

"How about a drink?" Connie's father offered. "Take the chill off." Before anyone answered him, he'd gone to the sideboard where the bottles were kept. "You gin drinkers?"

"That sounds good," the man said.

Connie's father made two drinks and gave one to the man and one to the wife. She took the glass and held it in the air, as if she were waiting for someone to take it from her.

One of the girls whispered something to her mother. The woman shook her head and told the girl she would have to wait. Connie was sure the girl wanted to use the bathroom. Didn't the woman think they had a bathroom?

"I'm cold," the little girl said.

Paula took the old crochet quilt from the back of her father's chair and tucked it around the girl as if she were one of Paula's baby dolls.

"That's so nice," the woman said, smiling at Paula the way teachers often smiled at the kids at school who got free breakfast, as if they wanted to give them so much more than their encouragement.

"Looks like we have a party all of the sudden," Connie's mother said. "An impromptu Christmas gathering." She went to refill her glass, and then turned on the CD player. She began to sway a little back and forth to the beat. "It's a strange night," she said. "An upside down night, isn't it?"

"I guess it is," the man said. "An inside out night."

"See? Tom gets it. Don't you, Tom?"

Connie's heart shrunk as she recognized the timbre of her mother's voice, the way she was too happy for the situation.

"How about a dance? Claude, dance with me," Connie's mother said.

"Not now," Connie's father said.

"Well, who needs you?" Connie's mother said, and she took Connie by the hands and began to dance with her. At first Connie was embarrassed, but when she saw that the girls on the couch were smiling, she felt suddenly graceful and pretty. She tried to follow along as her mother moved her around the room. Paula got excited and started dancing, waving her arms the way she had learned in the ballet class she'd taken the summer before at the YMCA.

"Mom? Dad?" It was Jean, standing on the stairs. She was wearing an old tee shirt and gym shorts that rose high up on her thighs.

"Jean! Come down!" Connie's mother said. She let go of one of Connie's hands and twirled Connie around. Connie got tangled up and she and her mother broke apart. Connie kept twirling and dancing for the girls.

"Stop it, Connie!' Jean said. "Stop it right now."

Connie stopped dancing. Suddenly, she realized that the girls were not smiling at her but that they were trying to hide their laughter. Connie felt humiliated. She looked at Jean, widened her eyes, giving Jean that signal that she needed to be saved. But Jean did not come to her rescue. Something in her face had shifted and Connie thought she was seeing a much older version of Jean, as if time had jumped ahead and here was Jean, maybe someone's wife, maybe somebody's mother, maybe living somewhere very far away. And in that moment, Connie had the idea that she wouldn't know Jean when they were older, that when Jean left the family, she would leave Connie, too, because Connie would remind her of things she didn't want to remember.

«» «» «»

The snow stopped sometime during the night and the sky was so bright that when Connie looked outside the kitchen window, her eyes grew teary. She poured out the bowls of cereal and then Jean came into the kitchen, carrying the glasses that had been left in the living room. She walked carefully, the three empty glasses in one hand and the full one in the other. The clear liquor threatened to spill over the rim, but Jean managed to get the glasses onto the counter in time. While Connie washed the glasses, Jean put together Paula's lunch.

On the way to school, the girls stopped to watch a tow truck driver working to hook a station wagon to his truck. The high whine of his winch sang out into the brisk morning as the back end of the car tilted up higher and higher. Skis crowded the windows of the station wagon. It had been nearly two in the morning when the taxi had finally arrived to take the family to the fire station.

The tow truck maneuvered back and forth until the car broke free of the snow bank. When the truck drove off, the car followed along like an unwilling child. Connie realized that had the car not become stuck, it would have gone off the edge of the road and fallen down the embankment that led towards the river. She remembered how fragile the ice had been the day before. Now she imagined the car sliding beneath the water, and the ski hats—blue, green, and yellow—floating out of the windows and rising to the surface, their tassels wavering atop the water like small flags, while below, the three girls sat in the back seat of the car holding hands. They would have been a help to one another, the way sisters can be. ▣

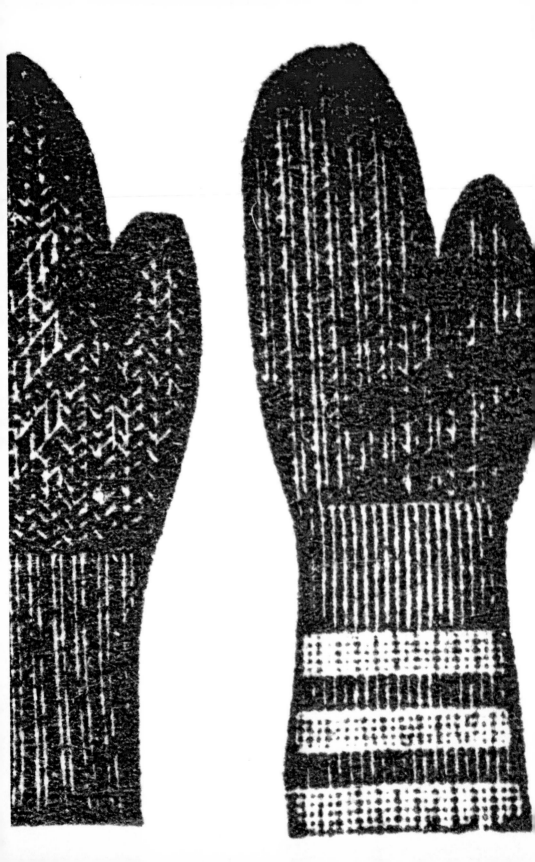

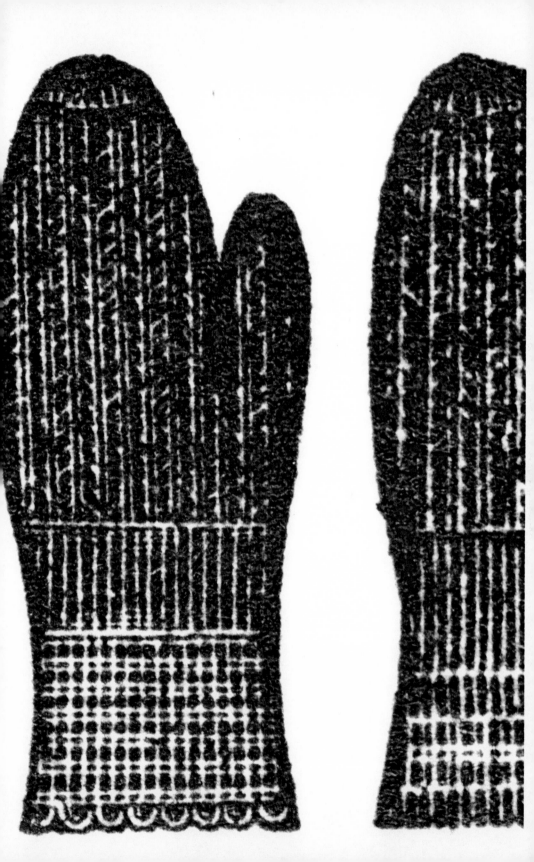

THE COWS

Lydia Davis

Each

new day, when they come out from the far side of the barn, it is like the next act, or the start of an entirely new play.

They come out from behind the barn as though something is going to happen, and then nothing happens.

They amble out from the far side of the barn with their rhythmic, graceful walk, and it is an occasion, like the start of a parade.

Or we pull back the curtain in the morning and they are already there, in the early sunlight.

Sometimes the second and third come out in stately procession while the first has stopped and stands still, staring.

They are a deep, inky black. It is a black that swallows light, like a black hole.

Their bodies are entirely black, but they have white on their faces. On the faces of two of them, there are large patches of white, like a mask. On the face of the third, there is only a small patch on the forehead, the size of a silver dollar.

They are motionless until they move again, one foot and then another—fore, hind, fore, hind—and stop in another place, motionless again.

So often they are standing completely still. Yet when I look up again a few minutes later, they are in another place, again standing completely still.

When they all three stand bunched together in a far corner of the field by the woods, they form one dark irregular mass, with twelve legs.

They are often crowded together in the large field. But sometimes they lie down far apart from each other, evenly spaced over the grass.

The third comes out into the field from behind the barn when the other two have already chosen their spots, quite far apart. She can choose to join either one. She goes deliberately to the one in the far corner. Does she prefer the company of that cow, or does she prefer that corner, or is it more complicated—that that corner seems more appealing because of the presence of that cow?

Their attention is complete, as they look across the road: they are still, and face us, full face.

Just because they are so still, their attitude seems philosophical.

I see them most often out the kitchen window over the top of a hedge. My view of them is bounded on either side by leafy trees. I am surprised that they are so often visible, because the portion of the hedge over which I see them is only about three feet long, and, even more puzzling, if I hold my arm straight out in front of me, the field of my vision in which they are grazing is only the length of half a finger. Yet that field of vision contains a part of their actual grazing field that is hundreds of square feet in area.

That one's legs are moving but because she is facing us directly she seems to be staying in one place. Yet she is getting bigger, so she must be coming this way.

They are sometimes a mass of black, a lumpy black clump against the snow, with a head at either end and many legs below.

Or: the three of them, seen from the side, when they are all facing the same way, three deep, make one thick cow with three heads, two up and one lowered.

In an access of emotion, she trots a few feet.

Against the snow, in the distance, coming head-on this way, separately, spaced far apart, they are like wide black strokes of a pen.

Sometimes they function as a single entity, as when they walk forward in a group, in little relays.

One gains courage from the one in front of her and moves forward a few steps, passing her by just a little. Now the one farthest back gains courage from the one in front and moves forward until she, in turn, is the leader. And so in this way, taking courage from each other, they advance, as a group, toward the strange thing in front of them.

In this, they are not unlike the small flock of pigeons we sometimes see over the railway station, wheeling and turning in the sky, making immediate small group decisions about where to go next.

Two of them are standing close together: now they both move at the same moment, shifting into a different position in relation to each other, and then stand still again, as if following exactly the instructions of, say, a choreographer.

Now they shift so that there is a head at either end and two thick leg-clusters in between.

They are so still, and their legs so thin, in comparison to their bodies, that sometimes their legs seem like prongs, and they are stuck to the earth.

In a moment of solitary levity, as she leads the way out across the field, she bucks once and then prances.

They are so black on the white snow and standing so close together that I don't know if there are three there together, or just two—but surely there are more than eight legs in that bunch?

Today, two appear halfway out from behind the barn, standing still. Ten minutes go by. Now they are all the way out, standing still. Another ten minutes go by. Now the third is out and they are all three in a line, standing still.

Two of them are beginning a lively game of butt-your-head when a car goes by and they stop to look.

At a distance, one bows down into the snow; the other two watch, then begin to trot toward her, then break into a canter.

Her head, from the side, is nearly an isosceles triangle, with a blunted corner where her nose is.

After staying with the others in a tight clump for some time, one walks away by herself to the far corner of the field: at this moment, she does seem to have a mind of her own.

Lying down, seen from the side, her head up, feet bent in front of her, she forms a long, very acute triangle.

She bucks, stiffly rocking back and forth. This excites another one to butt heads with her. After they are done butting heads, the other one puts her nose back down to the ground and this one stands still, looking straight ahead, as though wondering what she just did.

Forms of play: head butting; mounting, either at the back or at the front; trotting away by yourself; trotting together; going off bucking and prancing by yourself; resting your head and chest on the ground until they notice and trot toward you; circling each other; taking the position for head-butting and then not doing it.

She moos toward the wooded hills behind her, and the sound comes back. She moos in a high falsetto before the note descends abruptly, or she moos in a falsetto that does not descend. It is a very small sound to come from such a large, dark animal.

Today, they are positioned exactly one behind the next in a line, head to tail, as though coupled like the cars of a railway train, the first looking straight forward like the headlight of the locomotive.

They are often like a math problem: 2 cows lying down in the snow plus 1 cow standing up looking at the hill equals 3 cows.

Or: 1 cow lying down in the snow plus 2 cows on their feet looking this way across the road equals 3 cows.

Today, they are all three lying down.

The shape of a black cow, seen directly head-on: a smooth black oval, larger at the top and tapering at the bottom to a very narrow extension, like a tear drop or raindrop upside down.

Standing with their back ends close together, now, they face three of the four cardinal points of the compass.

Sometimes one takes the position for defecating, and her tail, raised, has the curved shape of a pump handle.

Now, because it is winter, they are not grazing, but only standing still and staring, or walking here and there, now and then.

How often they stand still and look around as though they have never been here before.

They are nearly the same size, and yet one is the largest, one the middle-sized, and one the smallest.

One of them is in the foreground and two are farther back, in the middle ground between her and the woods. In my field of vision, she occupies the same amount of space in the foreground as they occupy together in the middle ground.

They seem expectant this morning, but it is a combination of two things: their alert expressions, as they listen to a loud woodpecker; and the strange yellow light before a storm.

How flexible, and how precise, she is: she can reach one of her back hoofs all the way forward, to scratch a particular spot inside her ear.

They do not know the words "person," "neighbor," "watch," or even "cow."

A winter's day: first, a boy plays in the snow in the same field as the cows.

Then, outside the field, three boys throw snowballs at a fourth boy who rides past them on a bike.

Meanwhile, the three cows are standing end to end, each touching the next, like paper cutouts.

Now the boys begin to throw snowballs at the cows. A neighbor watching says: "It was only a matter of time. They were bound to do it sooner or later."

But the cows merely walk away from the boys.

It has been snowing heavily for some time, and it is still snowing. When we go up to them, where they stand by the fence, we see that there is a layer of snow on their backs. There is also a layer of snow on their faces, and even a thin line of snow on each of the whiskers around their mouths. The snow on their faces is so white that the white patches on their faces, which once looked so white against their black, now seem to be a shade of yellow.

It is the lowered head that makes her seem less noble than, say, a horse, or a deer surprised in the woods. More exactly, it is her lowered head and neck. As she stands still, her head is level with her back, or even a little lower, and so she seems to be hanging her head in discouragement, embarrassment, or shame. There is at least a suggestion of humility and dullness about her. But all these suggestions are false.

He says to us: they don't really do anything. But it is true that there is not a lot for them to do.

At the far edge of the field, next to the woods, they are walking from right to left, and because of where they are in the field, their dark bodies entirely disappear against the dark woods behind them, while their legs are still visible against the snow—black sticks twinkling against the white ground.

Grace: as they walk, they are more graceful when seen from the side than they are when seen from the front. Seen from the front, as they walk, they tip just a little from side to side.

When they are walking, their forelegs are more graceful than their back legs, which appear stiffer.

Does she lie down because the other two have lain down before her, or are they all three lying down because they all feel it is just the right time to lie down? (It is just after noon, on a chilly early spring day, with intermittent sun and no snow on the ground.)

Is the shape of her lying down, when seen from the side, most of all like a boot-jack as seen from above?

It is hard to believe a life could be so simple, but it is just this simple. It is the life of a ruminant, a protected domestic ruminant. If she were to give birth to a calf, though, her life would be more complicated.

The forelegs are more graceful than the back legs because they lift in a curve, whereas the back legs lift in a jagged line like a bolt of lightning.

But perhaps the back legs, while less graceful than the forelegs, are more elegant.

It is because of the way the joints in the legs work: whereas the two lower joints of the front leg bend the same way, so that the front leg as it is raised forms a curve, the two lower joints of the back leg bend in opposite directions, so that the leg, when raised, forms two opposite angles, the lower one gentle, pointing forward, the upper one sharp, pointing back.

The cows in the past, the present, and the future: they were so black against the pale yellow-green grass of late November. Then they were so black against the white snow of winter. Now they are so black against the tawny grass of early spring. Soon they will be so black against the dark green grass of summer.

Because there are three, one of them can watch what the other two are doing together.

Or, because there are three, two can worry about the third, for instance the one lying down. They worry about her even though she often lies down, and even though they all often lie down. Now the two worried ones stand at angles to the other, with their noses down against her, until at last she gets up.

The angles of a cow as she grazes, seen from the side: from her tail to her shoulder, there is a very gradual, barely perceptible slope, then, from her shoulder to the tip of her nose, down in the grass, a very steep slope.

The position, or form, itself, of the grazing cow, when seen from the side, is graceful.

Why do they so often graze side-view on to me, rather than front- or rear-view on? Is it so that they can keep an eye on both the woods, on one side, and the road, on the other? Or does the flow of traffic on the road, sparse though it is, right to left, and left to right, influence them so that they graze parallel to it?

Or perhaps it isn't true that they graze more often sideways on to me. Maybe I simply pay more attention to them when they are sideways on. After all, when they are perfectly sideways on, to me, the greatest surface area of their bodies is visible to me; as soon as the angle changes, I see less of them, until, when they are perfectly end-on or front-on to me, the least of them is visible.

They make slow progress here and there in the field, with only their tails moving briskly from side to side. In contrast, little flocks of birds—as black as they are—fly up and land constantly in waves behind and around them. The birds move with what looks to us like joy or exhilaration but is probably simply keenness in pursuit of their prey—the flies that in turn dart out from the cows and land on them again.

Their tails do not exactly whip or flap, and they do not swish, since there is no swishing sound. There is a swooping or looping motion to them, with a little fillip at the end, from the tasseled part.

When we come close to them, they are curious and come forward. They want to look at us and smell us. They blow out, forcefully, to clear their passages, before they smell us.

They like to lick—a person's hand or sleeve, or the withers or back of another cow. They like to be licked: while she is being licked, she stands very still with her head slightly lowered and a look of deep concentration in her eyes.

One may be jealous of another being licked: she thrusts her head under the outstretched neck of the one licking, and butts upward till the licking stops.

Just as it is hard for us, in our garden, to stop weeding, because there is always another weed there in front of us, it may be hard for her to stop grazing, because there are always a few more shoots of fresh grass just ahead of her.

If the grass is short, she may bite it directly with her teeth; if the grass is longer, she may capture it first with a sideways sweeping motion of her tongue, in order to bring it into her mouth.

Their large tongues are not pink. The tongues of two of them are light gray. The tongue of the third, the darkest one, is dark gray.

Other neighbors may be away, from time to time, but the cows are always there, in the field. Or, if they are not in the field, they are in the barn.

And I know that if they are in the field, and if I go up to the fence on this side, they will, all three, sooner or later come up to the fence on the other side, to meet me.

I see only one cow, by the fence. As I walk up to the fence, I see part of a second cow: one ear sticking sideways out the door of the barn. Soon, I know, her whole face will appear, looking at me.

At dusk, when our light is on indoors, they can't be seen, though they are there in the field across the road. If we turn off the light, and look into the dusk, gradually they can be seen again.

They are still out there, grazing, at dusk. But as the dusk turns to dark, while the sky above the woods is still a purplish blue, it is harder and harder to see their black bodies against the darkening field. Then they can't be seen at all, but they are still out there, grazing in the dark. ▣

CONTRIBUTORS

Lydia Davis, a 2003 MacArthur Fellow, is the author of VARIETIES OF DISTURBANCE, which was a National Book Award Finalist, SAMUEL JOHNSON IS INDIGNANT, ALMOST NO MEMORY, THE END OF THE STORY, and BREAK IT DOWN. Her new book, COLLECTED STORIES, has just been published by Farrar, Straus & Giroux. Her work has appeared in *Conjunctions*, *Harper's*, *The New Yorker*, *Bomb*, *The Paris Review*, *Tin House*, *McSweeney's*, and many other magazines and literary journals. Davis is a translator of the French works by Maurice Blanchot and Michael Leiris, as well as a highly-acclaimed new translation of Marcel Proust's SWANN'S WAY for Penguin Classics. Among other honors, she has been awarded a Guggenheim Fellowship and a Lannan Literary Prize, and has been named Chevalier of the Order of Arts and Letters by the French Government. In 2003, she won the French-American Translation Prize, and in 2005 she was inducted into the Academy of Arts & Sciences. She lives in upstate New York with her family.

Pasha Malla is the author of THE WITHDRAWAL METHOD (stories) and ALL OUR GRANDFATHERS ARE GHOSTS (poems, sort of). He is currently at work on a novel.

Stephen O'Connor is the author of RESCUE, short fiction and poetry; WILL MY NAME BE SHOUTED OUT?, memoir and social criticism; ORPHAN TRAINS, narrative history, and HERE COMES ANOTHER LESSON, short fiction, forthcoming from Free Press. His fiction and poetry have been in *The New Yorker, Poetry Magazine, Conjunctions, TriQuarterly, Threepenny Review, New England Review, The Missouri Review, The Quarterly, Partisan Review*, and many other places. His essays and journalism have appeared in *The New York Times, DoubleTake, The Nation, AGNI, The Chicago Tribune, The Boston Globe,* and elsewhere. He is a recipient of the Cornell Woolrich Fellowship in Creative Writing from Columbia University; the Visiting Fellowship for Historical Research by Artists and Writers from the American Antiquarian Society; and the DeWitt Wallace/Reader's Digest Fellowship from the MacDowell Colony. He teaches fiction and nonfiction writing in the MFA programs of Columbia and Sarah Lawrence.

Marisa Silver made her fictional debut in The New Yorker when she was featured in that magazine's first "Debut Fiction" issue. Her collection of short stories, BABE IN PARADISE was published by W.W. Norton in 2001, and named a *New York Times* Notable Book of the Year and was a *Los Angeles Times* Best Book of the Year. In 2005, W.W. Norton published her novel, NO DIRECTION HOME. Her latest novel, THE GOD OF WAR, was published in 2008 by Simon and Schuster, and is a finalist for the *Los Angeles Times* Book Prize for fiction. Her fiction has been anthologized in *The Best American Short Stories* and in *The O. Henry Prize Stories.* A new collection of stories will be published in April, 2010.

Colson Whitehead, a 2002 MacArthur Fellow, is the author of four novels and a book of essays about New York City. His most recent book is SAG HARBOR.

CPSIA information can be obtained at www.ICGtesting.com
Printed in the USA
BVOW012301210113

311222BV00001B/32/P